MAX AND THE
MULTIVERSE

Book One

A novel by Zachry Wheeler

ISBN: 978-0-9982049-2-5
Edited by Jennifer Amon
ZachryWheeler.com

* Gold Medal Winner - Global Ebook Awards
* Finalist - National Indie Excellence Awards
* Finalist - Next Generation Indie Book Awards
* Finalist - Dante Rossetti Book Awards
* Finalist - Best Book Awards
* Finalist - NMAZ Book Awards

When writing humor, there are a few ways to do it right and a million ways to do it wrong. This book is dedicated to Douglas Adams, my literary hero.

CHAPTER 1

Max stared at a dingy basement wall, tracing the grout lines of bare cinder blocks. He stood motionless in the center of the room, silent and waiting. Nostrils flared as they recycled the stale air. Fingernails scraped on tattered jeans. A pair of dim lamps painted haunting shadows on a cracked ceiling. His eyes shifted towards every faint sound. A thump here, a muffle there, followed by footsteps. Loud clomps overhead, then down the hall, then nothing. Silence ensnared the room. A door slammed. A car started soon after and faded into the distance. Max closed his eyes, took a measured breath, then scared the crap out of his cat by shouting "Spring break!"

Max's parents had departed for Hawaii, leaving him to fend for himself in the dusty suburbs of Albuquerque, New Mexico. Not that he minded. As an only child with social anxieties and a crippling fear of the outdoors, he welcomed a quiet week in a dank basement. He enjoyed it, preferred it even. Spring break to most teens meant travel to exotic locales, or at the very least, anywhere but home. Max had no interest in such things. Spring break to him meant one thing: gaming, lots and lots of gaming, an endless romp of caffeinated carnage without curfews or prying parents.

And so, it began.

His closest friends inhabited pixels on a computer, the avatars of fleshy cohorts all around the world. They escaped their real-life dungeons by slaughtering monsters in virtual ones. It gave them a sense of pride and accomplishment, all while dismantling their basic social faculties. Two days into an epic bender, Max's cat found him facedown and drooling on a rather expensive keyboard.

"Oi, Max. Time to get up."

"Huh?" Max stirred at his desk.

"Arise, you lazy sod. I'm hungry."

"Okay, okay, I'll—wait, *what?*"

Max opened his eyes to find a chubby orange tabby with green eyes and puffy jowls sitting on the desk beside him, part one of a reliable morning routine. However, the usual crop of impatient meows had been replaced by the King's English, complete with a disarming British accent.

"Morning," Ross said.

Max yelped and flung himself backwards, tumbling out of the chair. His body thumped the cold tile floor and rolled to a rest against the couch. The chair clanked and clattered before landing on its side. Max whipped a frightened gaze to an apathetic feline.

"That looked painful," Ross said.

Max flinched.

Ross raised an eyebrow while maintaining a ninja-like stillness, conveying the least possible amount of concern. "You okay there, mate?"

"You can talk. You're *talking.*"

"Yeah, so?"

"But how? You don't, um, I mean ..." Max's sputtering mind sifted through a deluge of questions before settling on the most impractical one. "Do all cats talk?"

"What, do you mean figuratively?"

Max started to respond, then stopped, then started and stopped again. His brain and mouth refused to cooperate, sounding like a faulty video stream.

"Ooookay then, moving on. You're awake. I'm hungry. Get off

the damn floor, get your head on straight, and meet me in the kitch-en." Ross dropped from the desk and trotted towards the stairs.

Max shook his head and blinked several times, trying to offload the hallucination. He untangled himself and leaned back against the couch. After a scowl and shoulder roll, he pressed a finger to his neck to check his pulse, explaining a grand total of nothing.

An annoyed Ross peeked around the stairwell. "Are you coming or not?"

Max flinched again and covered his heart. "Jeez, give me a mi-nute."

"That's another minute I have to abide an empty belly, now get a move on. By the way, the litter pan is full and I deuced in the bath-tub. You might want to address that after you tend to my nutritional needs."

Max responded with a contorted gaze.

Ross huffed and scampered up the stairs.

Max slapped himself across the cheek, winced in pain, and im-mediately regretted the decision. Climbing to his feet, he glanced over to a morning sunbeam peeking through a small port window, then grimaced like an albino cave troll. Designed as a mother-in-law suite, the basement featured a bathroom, kitchenette, and external entry, allowing Max to come and go as he pleased, not that it mattered much. His real-world obligations peaked at school and the occasional girlfriend, so he preferred to stay put, content to explore his virtual worlds under a veil of darkness.

He spent most of his time in a living room of sorts, in the sense that it housed the evidence of something living. Apart from an ex-travagant gaming system, furnishings amounted to little more than a squatter's paradise. A ratty couch and rickety table served as bed-room and dining room. Corners and cubbies seemed hell-bent on expanding an impressive collection of dust bunnies. A pair of parti-cleboard bookcases with opposing veneers gave a firm middle finger to interior design. An assortment of comic books, computer manuals, and gadget boxes completed the portrait of a standard nerd cave.

Max climbed the stairs like a half-naked camp counselor in a horror movie. He paused at the top and peered around the doorframe, scanning the hallway through widened eyes. Everything seemed in order, down to the forced smiles of family pictures along the walls. He tiptoed down the hall, pausing to examine each passing room. When he arrived at the end, he poked his head into a sage green kitchen where hanging pots reflected the morning sunlight. Ross stood in the center of the room with an expectant gaze.

Max froze and gawked at the feline.

Ross sighed. "Um, food? Sometime around *now* would be nice."

Max stiffened his posture and crept towards the pantry while maintaining eye contact.

Ross tilted his head. "You're starting to weird me out a bit."

Max filled a bowl with cat food, lowered it to the floor, and slid it over to Ross.

"Thanks, mate. And for the record, that was way more than a minute." Ross plunked his face into the bowl, spilling bits of kibble onto the floor.

Max backed away slowly like a vegan at a hog roast. He turned to the sink, cranked the faucet, and splashed his face with cold water. Droplets fell from his dangling jaw as he gazed out the window at nothing in particular. After a brief mental reboot, his attention shifted to the coffee maker, the lifeblood of any true gamer. He fixed a pot, filled his favorite mug, and lowered himself to the kitchen table. Sip after sip, he studied his furry friend while fretting over mental health and conversation etiquette. Small talk proved vexing with other humans, let alone with a cognizant pet. Convinced he was dreaming, or perhaps the target of an elaborate prank, Max decided to test the waters with a civil exchange.

"So, um, any plans for the day?"

Ross halted mid-chew and lifted an irked face from the bowl. "What, besides eating?" he said through a mouthful of kibble.

"Yeah, I guess."

"Why?" Ross narrowed his eyes.

"I don't know, just curious."

"Okay. I'll play your little mind game."

"It's not a game. I'm just making conversation."

"Life is a never-ending game of attrition. Our wits, swords. Our composure, shields."

Max rolled his eyes. "Jeez, dude. It's a simple, harmless, superficial question. I don't need a Shakespearian response."

"Fine." Ross thought for a moment while crunching. "I haven't thought much past this bowl, to be honest. Napping will be a high priority, on a variety of precarious surfaces. Might take in a window viewing or chase some sunbeams. May freak the hell out for no apparent reason, that's always fun." He ruffled his brow. "Why? Is there anything I should know about?"

"Nothing comes to mind. Why are you so suspicious?"

"That trollop of a girlfriend isn't coming over, is she?"

"Who, Megan?"

"No, Miley Cyrus. Who the bloody hell do you think I mean?"

"No need to be a dick about it. What's wrong with her coming over?"

"Well, duh, she's an insufferable twit."

"Wow." Max cringed. "That's a bit harsh. I thought you liked her."

"What? When did I ever give you that impression?"

"So you *don't* like her?"

Ross huffed and glanced away for a moment. "You are one dense wanker, you know that? How many times do we need to have this conversation?"

Max started to respond, but sighed instead.

"She's a canine sympathizer, Max. She consistently reeks of wet dog and utterly fails to grasp the concept of an inside voice. I have choked down her prattle for long enough. Let it be known that I am very close to a rash retaliation."

"Please don't. She's a good person."

"Seriously, the next time I see that dimwitted bint, I'm going to vomit in her shoes."

"Fine, no Megan today." Max groaned and rubbed his forehead. "Jeez, it's like living with a douchebag Garfield."

"That's racist." Ross cocked his ears back.

"What? How is that— You're both—" Max paused for a brain buffer. He shook his head, took another sip of coffee, then stood from the table. "I'm going out to get the mail."

Ross replied with a stink eye, then plunked his face back into the bowl.

Max shuffled to the front door, unlatched it with a limp hand, and greeted an onslaught of New Mexican sunlight. The heat needled his pale skin as he lumbered towards the street with an arm raised overhead. He grabbed a handful of letters from the mailbox, sifted through a pile of mostly junk, then turned for the house.

"Maximus!" said a voice from below.

"Sweet mother of pancakes!" Max convulsed the letters out of his hands.

"Sorry mate, didn't mean to wonk you," the voice said, also in a British accent.

Max palmed his heaving chest. He glanced down to find the cheerful face of Gerald, the neighbor's cat, a dirty brown tabby with blue eyes and an obvious weight problem.

"You got any more of those salmon treats? I could really go for some."

"Shut up, minger," Ross said from an open windowsill. "You need treats like a Max needs a third willy."

Gerald scrunched his brow. "You have *two* knobs?"

"No, of course not," Max said, then glared at Ross.

Gerald perked. "My uncle had one eye, three legs, and talked like a pirate. True story. Strange lad, that one."

Ross snorted with amusement.

Max gathered the letters from the ground and stomped towards the front door with Gerald prancing behind.

"About those trea—" Gerald said as the door slammed in his face.

Max tossed the mail onto the counter, scowled at Ross, then flopped back into his chair.

Ross snickered and returned to his food bowl.

Max leaned forward and folded his hands on the table. Troubled eyes stared at the surface as he nodded with the steady cadence of a metronome. Fluttering breaths fled his lungs with every sip of coffee. Teeth chattered behind taut lips, filling his mind with a grim melody. After a long spell of nervous contemplation, he dropped his forehead to the table with a loud thump.

Ross jerked away from the bowl with cocked ears and a poofed tail. "What the hell, man?"

"I'm crazy, I'm crazy, I'm crazy," Max said from beneath an arm fort.

"What do you mean *crazy*?"

Max lifted his head and heaved with a mounting panic attack, his unhinged gaze darting around the room. "I've gone insane. My cat is talking to me. My damn cat, and as Nigel Puffbottom no less." Writhing and panting, he closed his eyes and tucked his arms to regain some composure. "I must be dreaming, or sleepwalking, or something. My brain has lost its footing and I'm just imagining cats talking to me. That's all. I'm okay. I'm okay. I'm perfectly fine."

"Brains can't have a footing," Ross said with a flat tone.

Max huffed and opened his eyes. "You can be a real jerk, you know that? Or not, who knows, it's all in my head."

"So, you don't think I'm talking right now?"

"Of course not, cats don't talk."

Ross uncocked his ears and pondered the declaration. He pranced over to the nearest chair, bounded up to the table, and settled in front of Max. After a brief silence, he turned towards the window. "Oi, Gerald!"

Gerald's head popped up from beneath the windowsill. "All right, Ross?"

"Get this, Max says that cats don't talk."

"What, does he mean figuratively?"

"No, he says not at all."

"Well that's interesting because we're having a lovely conversation."

"Exactly my point."

7

"That doesn't prove a damn thing," Max said through a double facepalm.

"Wow, what's his damage today?" Gerald said to Ross.

"Don't know, trying to figure that out."

"Well, I'll leave you to it then. Best of luck."

"Cheers, Gerald."

Gerald ducked away as Ross returned his gaze.

Max glared at him through a finger fence.

"Don't give me that look. I'm trying to help you."

"Help me?" Max slapped his hands on the table. "How on Earth is that helping?"

"Fine, my apologies. Truce." Ross bowed his head for a moment, then lifted onto his hind legs. He cleared his throat and dropped his voice to a smooth baritone. "The truth is ... you are the chosen one."

Max scrunched his brow. "Huh? What the hell are you talking about?"

"While I appreciate my given name of Rosco P. Coltrane on this planet, my real name is Reginald Sarcoga, first son of Hackamore. I hail from an ancient order of supreme beings that occupied the Zynfall Galaxy of Hamonrye. We settled upon your planet long ago and assumed the feline form to aid in our divine quest. I have spent my entire life looking for you. Today, we present ourselves to Your Grace. You are the one the prophecies foretold. You are the fabled Shifter, The Light, the vessel that will unite all universes under an infinite era of peace." Ross placed his paw on top of Max's hand. "It is time to fulfill your destiny, star child."

Max donned the bewildered expression of a preteen boy seeing his first pair of boobs. An eyelid twitched for good measure as his brain processed the reveal. With a renewed vitality, he locked eyes with a stoic Ross. "I knew it. I knew there was something bigger going on here. I have always felt the draw of some higher purpose."

"I am *so* pulling your leg right now." Ross smirked and removed his paw.

Max drooped with the sting of embarrassment. "You're such an asshole." He closed his eyes and thumped his head back onto the table.

"Gerald!" Ross said to the open window.

"Wotcha?" Gerald said as he popped his head up.

"I told him he was a star child with a destiny."

"Oh, that's cheeky. How'd he take it?"

"Not well. He keeps banging his head on the table."

"Won't that churn his noggin?"

"Can't break what's already broke."

"Brilliant, carry on then."

Max stood in a hurry, flinging his chair halfway across the kitchen. He rushed over to the window where a smiling Gerald perked with attention.

"So how about those trea—" Gerald said as the window slammed shut, muffling his voice behind the glass. "Right, shall I just bugger off then?"

Max ignored him, dropped the shade, and returned to the kitchen. He swiped the mug from the table and snapped at Ross. "You proud of yourself?"

"A touch, yeah."

Max downed a final swig before grabbing the pot for a refill. He sighed with defeat, then leaned back on the counter and stared at the floor. "So that's it, then. I'm nuttier than a squirrel turd."

"Yeah, you're probably schizophrenic or something."

Max sneered at Ross. "Thanks, you're so helpful."

"Oh c'mon mate, lighten up. Most people slog through life without ever knowing the wonders of true insanity. I say enjoy the pink elephants while you got 'em."

"Well, that's one terrible way to look at it."

Max spent the rest of the day coping like a normal teen, by avoiding the problem and turning to gaming. He battled digital demons while trying to ignore the color commentary of a sentient feline. Though unnerving, he did learn a great deal about life as a house cat. He learned that laser pointers were the purest of evils, that sunbeams healed every possible ailment, and that squirrels were a bunch of frolicking asshats that needed to be taught a lesson.

* * *

In another universe, about three and a half billion to the left, a small freighter ship exited hyperspace just outside of Neptune's orbit. As little more than a flying dumpster, the ship was not winning any beauty pageants. Its clunky hull appeared more mangled than designed, leaving one to suspect that its architect loved booze and Legos. A charcoal gray exterior with numerous dents and rust stains conveyed an impressive amount of disregard. The deep blue glow of its twin rear engines created a drab silhouette, like a bloated bat crossing a moonlit sky.

Apart from a standard registry code engraved in white lettering, the mundane craft carried no markings or obvious identifications, a calculated necessity for the crew. Its banal presence concealed a sophisticated collection of technology, including a military-grade frame, enhanced jump drive, and several pieces of plasma weaponry. To an average passerby, the ship read as little more than a poor drifter shuttle. After all, members of the PCDS (Precious Cargo Delivery Service) needed to guard their inconspicuousness above all else.

The sleek cockpit gleamed with an array of touch-based circuitry. A double-crescent control panel pinged with scans and alerts. Blinking blues and pulsing purples outlined the freighter's commander in the pilot seat, a shrewd Mulgawat by the name of Zoey Bryx. Most knew her by an ominous nickname: The Omen, earned for her distinct reputation as one of the most ruthless and efficient PCDS couriers to have ever lived.

When Zoey accepted a job, it came with an unwavering promise: *If I'm not on time, you can assume I'm dead.* Despite her young age, a twentysomething by Earth years, she won tremendous fame through an unrivaled dependability. As a result, she often found herself entrusted with some of the most extraordinary artifacts in all of existence, current cargo included. Nothing explicit, just a small plastic box with an address and the following instructions: *Handle with care, the great bag of marbles depends on it.* It rested inside a bio-lock safe at the rear of the cargo bay.

On their way to the Andromeda Galaxy, Zoey and her longtime girlfriend, a fellow Mulgawat and gifted machinist by the name of Perra Harbin, decided to make a pit stop at a boring yellow star. To anyone in the know, the destination was obvious. This particular star anchored a solar system famous for one of the universe's most delectable sources of water: a small icy moon named Europa orbiting a massive gas giant named Jupiter. Those fortunate enough to sample Europan water, harvested from enormous freshwater oceans far beneath its surface, often described it as a transcendent experience akin to licking a firetooth sandworm.

Zoey narrowed her deep blue eyes as she scanned the panoramic viewport. She slipped off her worn leather jacket and draped it across the back of the pilot seat, leaving her to the comfort of a thin tank top and cargo pants. A few taps of the control panel produced a green hologram of the current solar system, brightening her sunburst orange complexion and dark blue lips. A small cursor blinked at the outer orbit, signifying their current location. She brushed her choppy black hair aside and tapped the pulsing icon. The hologram pinged in response and zoomed into Neptune's orbital path. She nodded and input a course correction. The ship pitched downward, lifting a massive blue horizon into view. A smile stretched across her face as Neptune's cobalt sheen engulfed the cabin.

"Perra sweetie, we're here!"

A squeal of delight echoed from the cargo bay as Perra darted up a narrow corridor towards the cabin. The studded straps and tarnished buckles of her machinist pants clanked along the metal walls. She emerged with a toothy smile and peered out the viewport. Her creamy orange hand pressed against the console as she leaned forward. A series of error pings rang around the cabin, prompting Zoey to fumble for corrections.

"Ugh, watch what you're doing," Zoey said.

"Sorry," Perra said. "I'm just so excited to see it." She stepped back from the panel and wiped her grimy hands on a simple halter top.

Zoey nabbed the back of Perra's neck and pulled down, planting a kiss on her buttery orange cheek. Perra's long auburn ponytail brushed Zoey's shoulders, tickling the thin blue scales running down her upper arms. Perra snickered and plopped into the co-pilot chair.

"I'm excited too, my love," Zoey said.

"So where is it?" Widened eyes scanned the vista, her deep purple irises floating in pools of white. "That doesn't look like Jupiter at all. At least, not what I remember from the coms."

"We're not there-there yet, just here." Zoey pointed at the hologram. "We're at the edge of the planetary system. This is a controlled area, so we can't jump in directly. We have to taxi in from outer orbit."

Perra huffed. "That means we still have a few pochs left to travel."

"That's nothing, we'll be there before you know it. Let's see ..." Zoey tapped across the console, highlighting some basic system info. "Okay, we have a yellow dwarf star with eight planets, four rocky, four gaseous. Jupiter is fifth from the star, first gas giant. We're just outside the eighth's orbit. That's Neptune." She pointed at the giant blue planet filling the viewport. "Taxi speed is set at 10 gamuts a mark, putting Jupiter at about 3,000 marks away. See? Not even a full poch. Plenty of time to relax and load up some languages."

Perra sighed. "Okay, fine. Let's just hope it's nothing too complicated."

Zoey and Perra were not speaking an Earth dialect when they arrived. As citizens of Mulgawat, a small planet in the Ursa Major Group, they spoke Korish as their native tongue. To human ears, a Korish conversation sounded like a couple of sleep-deprived frogs getting stabbed in the throat. When entering any new system with dominant forms of language, it was customary to install the major dialects before docking at a station.

Perra reached into a side compartment and withdrew a cylindrical device, silver in color with a simple control pad. She plugged it into the console, spawning a hologram panel of diction data. "Looks like we have three. Chinese, Spanish, and English." A quick swipe loaded the infuser. She plucked it from the dock, placed the business end to her temple, then pressed a red button at the other end. A whir, zot, and ping signaled a successful installation. She shivered away a chill, then handed the device to Zoey.

"Only three? Nice." Zoey repeated the process.

Now they were speaking English, the most comfortable of the three. Chinese felt too weird on the face and Spanish sounded too damn sexy to take seriously.

"So, just under a poch, eh?" Perra stood from her seat, slid her hands across Zoey's chest, and whispered into her ear. "That does give us plenty of time to ... relax."

Zoey smirked. She confirmed the trajectory, engaged the autopilot, and lifted to her feet. A wandering finger hooked Perra's belt and yanked her into a steamy embrace. Wet lips and muffled moans broke the dull hum of the main engines. Perra pulled away and motioned down the corridor with a subtle gesture. Zoey bit her lip and nodded, allowing Perra to back down the passage with her lover in tow. Hungering for each other, they disappeared into the bedchamber.

CHAPTER 2

The multiverse has always presented itself as a tantalizing yet unprovable theory. It lurks within the realms of fevered speculation, something for geeks to discuss in the uncool corners of parties. Nevertheless, Max was the second being in all of existence to uncover the truth: that an infinite number of parallel universes do, in fact, exist. The first to verify the multiverse theory was Rumac of the Suth'ra Society, but he didn't care enough to publish.

For the most part, parallel universes are unremarkable reprints of each other and it takes a keen eye to notice any difference at all. The only variation between one and the next might be to the mating habits of cannibalistic space slugs. But whenever Max shifted, it was to a variant of his particular domain. This is an apparent rule of shifting, but we're only monkeysacking here (the equivalent of "spitballing" in another universe).

Max acquired his incredible ability in perhaps the dumbest way imaginable. He gamed, a lot, enough to worry parents and alienate girlfriends. On the second day of a spring break all to himself, he pushed the limits of an epic gaming marathon. The sun rose, the sun set, midnight came and went. As dawn loomed, his mental janitor clocked out and killed the lights. His face crashed onto the keyboard and mashed a sequence of commands not seen since the dark warring days of Galwock 36. This random turd of logic just so happened to match one of the stasis functions sent between universes. It rocketed through the ether and collided with that code packet. The rebound imprinted onto Max's subconscious, an event so improbable that it makes winning the lottery while being struck by lightning seem like a typical Tuesday. At that most fortuitous of moments, his psyche switched universes. When he awoke, his cat spoke with a British accent. And from that day forward, Max shifted to a new world whenever he fell asleep.

* * *

Max awoke on his crumb-infested couch. The crackle of empty wrappers saluted his rise from the cushions. Tired eyes scanned the room for anything abnormal, uncovering little more than the usual grime and disregard. Motes of dust swirled in a morning sunbeam. A thin cloud of body odor and cheese poof dust teased his nostrils. He plucked his phone from the coffee table and tapped the surface.

10:42 a.m., Tuesday.

After a few blinks and face rubs, he glanced down to find Ross staring at him from the floor. Max flinched the phone out of his hand and stiffened with fright, initiating a tense game of vernacular chicken. Ross stood his ground, statuesque, refusing to vocalize the first move. Max took a deep breath and offered his concession.

"Morning," Max said, using a minimal amount of lip muscles.

"Meow," Ross said, declaring victory.

"Oh thank goodness." Max collapsed into the couch. "I thought I was batshit crazy."

"Meow," Ross said, demanding food service.

"Yeah, I need to get outside today. Maybe the lack of vitamin D is taking its toll." He sighed, rubbed his eyes, and stared at the ceiling for a minute. "You know, I could really go for some chimichangas."

"Meow," Ross said, pointing out that his selfish behavior had once again trumped the nutritional needs of his loyal companion, and that the declaration of chimichangas served as a callous attempt to mock said nutrition.

Without a stylistic care in the world, Max added a frayed hoodie to his lounging ensemble, hooked a pair of flip-flops, and embarked on a culinary expedition. He pulled his beat-up hatchback out of the driveway and set sail for his favorite diner across town. The bright New Mexican sunlight poured through the windshield, warming his chest and tightening his face. While humming along to the radio, he clued into an uncomfortable reality. The roads were empty. No car horns, no pedestrians, no traffic of any kind, only the dull rumble of the engine as it broke an eerie silence.

His phone erupted with a series of shrill tones, startling him to attention. He grabbed the device from the cup holder and read the flashing alert.

CODE ORANGE ... CODE ORANGE ...

Pulling to a stop at the next intersection, he peered in all directions but found no signs of life. "Uh, this is no bueno. Maybe I should get off the ro—"

A thunderous crash hit the roof. Tires exploded, glass shattered, everything metal bent and screamed. Max let out a blood-curdling shriek as he and his crumpled car lifted into the air. Huge black claws gripped the roofline above the doors, shifting and scraping with every upward surge. Max gawked at them in wide-eyed disbelief, his face mangled by panic. An ominous flapping sound revealed itself overhead, filling him with a dreadful curiosity. He leaned forward and glanced up through the shattered windshield. The resulting shock tossed him back into the seat.

"Code orange," he said, shaking his head. "Would it not have been slightly more informative to say, oh, I don't know, *PTERO-DACTYLS*?! Warning! Giant winged death lizards! Get off the goddamn roads!"

Max rage-punched the steering wheel over and over, blowing the car horn with every hit, which in turn angered the pterodactyl. The beast sank its claws deeper into the frame and let out a piercing screech. Metal creaked and moaned as bits of glass bounced around the cabin. Max received the message loud and clear. He threw his hands up in what seemed like a necessary apology, then proceeded to sulk inside his flying doom wagon. "Well, I must admit, this will make for one badass obituary."

A deafening boom echoed overhead and ended with a crackle of static. The blast shook the car from side to side, forcing the winged reptile to adjust its grip. Another boom followed. The pterodactyl screeched and abandoned its purchase. Max unleashed another blood-curdling shriek as the car plummeted towards the ground. He latched onto the steering wheel and pulled back, as if to will his car into a James Bond flying machine. Max's life passed before his eyes, yet he still managed to pout about it. Seconds from impact, a blue energy cocoon surrounded the crumpled car and slowed its descent into a comfortable hover. The car placed itself onto a well-manicured section of grass inside a local park.

Max, still clenching the steering wheel with a sweaty death grip, surveyed his new surroundings with horrified eyes. Soon thereafter, a dirty brown pickup truck pulled up to the curb near Max's location. A chubby fellow in a plaid shirt and overalls stepped out of the truck and sauntered over to the wreckage. The man scratched his bushy beard and adjusted his trucker's cap. A long silvery contraption hung around his shoulder, expelling ribbons of steam. Max fixated on the device as the man reached the car.

"Howdy," the man said in a casual Southern drawl.

Max responded with a twitching eye.

"First time taken, I reckon?" the man said.

Max barfed in the passenger seat.

The man chuckled. "Helluva ride, eh? You look decent though, any bumps or booboos?"

Max wiped his mouth, regained what little composure he had, and turned back to the man. "Why am I not dead?"

"Well, yer Safety Net seemed to work fine. Had it been glitchy or sump'n?"

"My ... Safety Net?"

"Yeah, Safety Net. You know, your car's anti-impact system."

The man shifted his beard and raised an eyebrow. "You feelin' okay, feller?"

"Oh, that, yes." Max tried to neutralize the conversation. "I heard some loud booms, and then I was falling, and—"

"Ah, yessir, sorry 'bout that." He cleared his throat. "I missed my first shot, but I got that wily bastard with a strong second. Dammit all to Hades, I never miss my first shot, but that dad-blasted critter ain't exactly regular. Kind of embarrassing to tell you the Lord's honest truth. Please don't mention that in my Angie's List review, should you choose to write one, which would be greatly appreciated. Here's my card." The man fished a business card from his shirt pocket and handed it to Max.

"Clear Skies Extermination," Max said, reading aloud.

"Best in the bidness." The man nodded with pride.

Max continued reading. "Hank Redwood, Owner and Operator."

"A pleasure to make your acquaintance." He extended his hand. "And you are?"

"Max."

Hank clamped down on his hand and shook with vigor, causing Max to wince in social and physical discomfort. The silvery device bounced around Hank's shoulder, reflecting sunlight into Max's eyes.

"What's that?"

"Oh, son, we just got these in." Hank's tone elevated with giddy excitement. He swung the device around to his front and gripped it proudly with both hands. "This here is the new Remington Skyscraper 3200, best bug zapper money can buy." The thin, cylindrical device extended about three feet in length with a pistol grip and collapsible stock. Lights, vents, and digital displays peppered the shaft.

"Bug zapper?"

"Well, that's what we call the anti-dino guns in the service. This one here has that new electroshock softening feature, a more humane way of prodding 'em about. That way they don't get those nasty singe marks like they used to. Keeps all the dino-rights people happy n' such."

A sharp whistle caught Hank's attention. He turned to find a flatbed truck rolling up to the curb with another earthy man hanging out of the window. After waving hello, he turned back to Max.

"Well alright, there's yer clean up. That's Larry. Good man. He'll take mighty fine care of ye." Hank stood there with an expectant pause, like a bellhop awaiting a tip.

Max read the body language and searched for his wallet while contemplating the appropriate gratuity for shooting a pterodactyl off the roof of one's car. Without the slightest of clues, he handed Hank a $20 bill.

Hank responded with a wide grin. "Well that's mighty generous. Thank you, sir."

"No, thank you. You do fine work."

"You have a blessed day now. And remember to review us on Angie's List."

Hank turned away and walked towards his dirty pickup truck. He exchanged brief pleasantries with Larry, who approached the crumpled car.

"Alrighty, sir, time to get out the car," said the slender and stubbled mechanic.

Max tried to open his buckled door, but ended up with a sore shoulder. After a few unsuccessful attempts, he lifted himself out of the window like a decrepit Bo Duke. Inept at window exits, he lost his balance and tumbled face-up onto the grass. Worried eyes surveyed the clear blue sky for more winged danger.

"Ha, I recognize those claw marks," Larry said, pointing at the door. "Looks like you got hit by ol' Stumpy. I figured he would have ventured south by now. Must be gettin' on in years."

"Stumpy?" Max lifted to his feet.

"Yeah, big feller, been around a while. Got his foot nipped when he tried to take a Mack truck, lost some claws. Not the brightest lizard of the bunch."

"Oh, that one," Max said, trying to appear normalized.

"This won't take me but a few minutes to clean up. You need a ride or do you have someone you can call?"

"I can make a few calls." Max glanced around the park to gauge his whereabouts. "Do I pay you now?"

"Naw, dino-related safety and clean up are covered by county taxes. First-timer I take it?"

"Yeah, first time." Max lifted his gaze to the sky.

"Ha, ye busted yer dino cherry." Larry chuckled. "Was Stumpy gentle?"

Max rubbed his shoulder and lowered a flattened face to Larry. "Not particularly."

"No offense, friend, just pokin' fun. Welp, step on back and I'll get on this." Larry examined the mangled car before returning to his flatbed truck.

Max walked to the nearest curb while texting Megan.

[Max] Got hit by Stumpy. I'm okay. Can I get a ride?

[Megan] What?! Ugh. Address?

[Max] Academy Hills Park, Layton Ave.

[Megan] On my way. 10 mins.

[Max] Thank you.

Max sighed. "Glad you're okay. Need anything? I love you, or something."

With a grunt of discomfort, Max lowered himself onto the curb. He wiped the sweat from his face and surveyed the park grounds. Tiny, clawed footprints crisscrossed the dirt patches, each split down the middle by shallow lines. A rush of insight caused him to open a browser on his smartphone and search for "dinosaurs." The mystery deepened. Page after page he scrolled, uncovering a wide variety of dino-specific services; animal control, pet sitting, home protection, exterminators, groomers, butchers, skin traders, and an impressive number of insurance companies.

Max stared at the pavement and mumbled to himself. "Okay, let's think about this logically. There has to be a rational explanation. It's not like they opened a Jurassic Park and didn't—" Max returned to his phone and searched for "Jurassic Park" in a movie database. No record. "Huh," he said while gnawing his lower lip.

Megan pulled up to the curb, but Max failed to notice due to a viral video of a baby stegosaurus on a skateboard. She gave him a good long half-second before laying on the car horn, jolting Max to attention.

"You coming, asshole?" Megan said.

Max jumped to his feet, grunted with pain, then jogged over to the passenger door and slipped inside. Megan sped off before he settled, slamming the door on his shoulder. He grimaced and swallowed any verbal complaint.

"Thank you so much for this," Max said, groveling.

She stared at the road and shook her head, refusing to make eye contact.

Maintaining a reasonable level of abasement, he bowed his head and spoke with a soft tone. "Did I do something wrong?"

Megan erupted with a well-rehearsed rant. "Who the hell gets snatched by Stumpy these days? Do you know how clumsy and stupid that reptile is? What the hell were you doing? Just driving down an empty street?"

"I wasn't thinking."

"No, hiking alone in T-rex country is not thinking. This was brain dead."

"You're right, I'm sorry."

"This never happened, by the way. My friends would never let me live it down."

"Who cares what they think?"

Megan glared at Max before mocking the voices of her friends. "Oh, you're dating that nitwit who got plucked by Stumpy? What, was he hitchhiking with a blindfold or just skipping naked in the desert?"

Max opened his mouth to respond, but sighed instead.

Not to be outdone, Megan sighed louder.

They shared a few minutes of awkward silence before Megan pulled into the driveway of Max's house. The car jerked to a stop, causing him to wince in pain. With a grunt of soreness, he stepped outside onto the concrete.

"You're welcome," Megan said with a curt tone.

Max shot her a sour glance and resisted slamming the door. He gave her a flaccid wave as she backed out of the driveway. Tires squeaked upon the pavement as she about-faced and sped down the street. Max scowled and rubbed his neck as the car turned a corner and disappeared.

"Meow," Ross said from an open windowsill, hurling an unsavory insult.

"You said it, buddy." Max turned and limped towards the front door.

* * *

Zoey and Perra lay in a post-coitus entanglement. Their contrasted orange skins melded into fleshy ribbons atop the dusky bed sheets. Facing each other with legs entwined, Perra ran her fingertips up and down Zoey's flank. Zoey stroked the matte blue scales on Perra's shoulders. Perra slid her hand around her lover's neck and pulled her into a kiss. Their dark blue lips blended as one for a blissful moment. Perra heaved her bare breasts in contentment.

"I can't believe it," Perra said, brushing a strand of hair behind her ear. "Soon we'll be sitting at the cluster-famous Astral Tear, sipping on Europa's finest while sampling the best of Earth's caviar." She closed her eyes, placed both hands atop her chest, and expelled a long sigh of gratitude. "Life is good." Lifting her eyelids, she offered a warm smile to Zoey. "And life with you is truly wonderful."

"Ditto, my love," Zoey said, returning the smile.

"Maybe we'll meet an actual Earthling."

"Ugh, why would you want to do that? They're such brash creatures."

"I don't know, curiosity I guess. They did invent duct tape after all."

"Yeah, their one lasting contribution to the 'verse."

"Hey now, I use that stuff all the time. It's magical."

"I know, it shows." Zoey pounded a fist on the rear wall, sending hollow echoes around the room.

Perra gasped and poked Zoey in the ribs, prompting an array of playful squeals. They wrestled with each other for a moment before ending with a kiss. Perra reached behind her head and patted the dark gray wall of the inner hull. "Don't listen to her, baby. You're a fine vessel. Duct tape is an enhancement, really."

"Mmhmm."

Perra flipped onto her stomach and rested her head on folded arms. "So what do you think it'll be like?"

"I don't know." Zoey shrugged and flipped onto her back, bringing a handful of sheets with her. "White and cold I guess."

"Duh, smartass. You know what I mean. I hope it isn't too touristy."

"I doubt it. Europa is an ancillary post and the water feature is very posh. It's more of a choice destination than a whim port. I think we'll be fine. Minimal riffraff."

"Good. I would love a quiet and romantic getaway. It's been so long."

"I know. I could really use a warm bath, a fuzzy robe, and some needless pampering."

"I bet the spa is nice."

"Yeah, and super expensive."

"We can afford it." Perra nuzzled up beside Zoey and interlocked arms. "How often do we get to do something like this?"

Zoey smiled and pulled Perra closer for another kiss. "Good point. I think we have earned the right to indulge in some of life's finer things."

Perra bit her lower lip and draped an arm across Zoey's chest. "Thank you, sweetie. You're too good to me, you know that?"

"You are beyond worth it, my love."

"And the cargo will be fine?"

"Oh yes. This is a pass-through system, nobody to worry about here."

CHAPTER 3

Max awoke to a dry mouth and the blank canvas of a dim ceiling. Having fallen asleep in his gaming chair again, he began the morning with a sore neck, and much to his surprise, *only* a sore neck. He awaited the inevitable onslaught of aches and pains, but nothing came. Shifting in the chair, he groaned and rubbed his eyes. A few lip smacks moistened a parched tongue. A weary arm reached for a cup of stale coffee resting beside the keyboard, but paused just before hooking the handle. He lifted both arms into the air and studied the unblemished skin of an inactive basement dweller. All bumps and bruises from the previous day had disappeared. He felt fine, well-rested even.

Refocusing his attention onto the computer, he bumped the mouse and roused the machine from its slumber. The last thing he remembered was reading an article about the hassles of raptors in your garden. But now, the article concerned rabbits. He re-skimmed the piece with the bewildered stare of a chameleon at a rave, but found no mention of raptors, only rabbits. He checked his phone. No previous alerts. He closed the article and searched for "dinosaurs" again. Links to archaeological websites filled the screen, along with museums and exhibits. Max leaned back in the chair and shook his head.

"What the effing eff ..."

He rubbed his forehead, then returned his attention to the screen. Eyes narrowed as a peculiar idiom emerged. He scooted forward in his chair and studied curious headlines like "Grand Opening Museum Wing Schedules" and "Been Discovered New Species Has." He clicked on an article and read through the content. Or at least, he tried to. Sentences seemed to follow a new set of grammatical rules. Halfway through the piece, his frustration blurted out the answer. "Why does everything read like Yoda-speak?" He paused, then rolled his eyes and flopped back into the chair. "So this is what I have to deal with today."

"Meow," Ross said while rubbing on Max's leg. Or in cat speak, *Attention I need. Scratch you must give.*

Max scratched Ross's head, who returned an appropriate amount of purr payment.

To test his theory, Max searched the web for *Star Wars* clips. And sure enough, Yoda delivered his famous lines in familiar conversational English. "You will not look as good when you reach 900 years old," the Jedi said, sounding more bitchy than wise. On the flip side, the other characters tossed around their cryptic word salads.

"Your father I am," Vader said.

"True that is not," Luke said.

"Up laugh it fuzzball," Han said.

"Argh arrrgh argarg," Chewbacca said, which sounded just fine.

As a result, many scenes lost the majority of their gusto, coming across as more of a space-themed soap opera.

Max's day involved meeting Megan and her friends for lunch, an obligation he now regretted. He and Megan shared a lot in common, from a general distaste of other people to an ongoing desire to mock said people. They bonded over a mutual misanthropy, despite hailing from opposite ends of the social spectrum. Their relationship persisted as a crude experiment, each using the other to satisfy raw desires and curiosity. On the other hand, they battled over a complete imbalance of priority. Megan, the very definition of shallow, needed a like-minded friend base in which to perpetuate her shallowness. Max hated each and every one of them, but he hated conflict even more, so he tolerated their presence to maintain peace.

Before heading out, Max spent the morning absorbing as much of the new language structure as he could. His mind struggled through clips and articles, deconstructing each line while resisting a potent urge to speak in a Yoda voice. He practiced by narrating activities.

"Dirty this bowl is. In sink I shall place it."

"Meow," Ross said. Or in cat speak, *Thrown up I have. Clean it you must.*

"Smelly this shirt is. In hamper I shall toss it."

"Meow," Ross said. Or in cat speak, *Stupid you sound.*

Max assembled some classier-than-usual geek attire, consisting of a plaid shirt, unsoiled jeans, and black Chucks. Pocketing his wallet and phone, he took one final look in the bathroom mirror and prepared himself for a day of linguistic battle. "Do or do not. There is no try," he said in his best Yoda voice. A brief chuckle melted into an annoyed sigh. After bidding farewell to his reflection, he swiped his keys from the counter and departed for the mall.

Max established a simple goal for lunch: talk as little as possible to as few people as possible. Gamers, as a reclusive subspecies of society, often found themselves relegated to the sidelines of social circles where discourse remained optional. Thus, the strategy seemed sound. Since the dawn of the Information Age, not a single gamer has expressed a desire for casual public interaction. Gaming has been, and always will be, a protected bastion of the socially awkward.

However, in order to remain in Megan's good graces, Max knew that he must suffer through some forced interaction. As an ungraceful geek, he understood that even the slightest variation on acceptable conversation stuck out like a sore thumb, like hearing a New York Italian use the term *y'all*. The brain found it disorienting and chided the ears for mishearing it. Max could only hope for minimal participation, knowing that the combination of gamer-speak and new grammar rules might render him as incoherent as a drunken Scotsman.

Max sat in the parking lot of an upscale mall, of course, and stared at the department store entrance through his car's windshield. The glare of the afternoon sun warmed his torso, but he failed to notice. His fingers rapped on the steering wheel, matching his galloping heartbeat. "Yoda for a day, you can do this. May the force be with you. Or rather, with you may the force be." His cheeks puffed with a series of quickened breaths, like a weightlifter preparing for an epic hoist. With a thump of his shoulder, he opened the car door, assumed his usual persona, and shuffled towards the front entrance.

A jittery hand hooked the door handle and swung it open. He made it three steps inside before meeting eyes with a cheerful greeter.

"G'morning, to Nordstrom welcome. Good weekend you have?"

Max froze and stared at her through a blank expression. The swinging door beat the sill over and over, like a metronome counting each second of awkwardness. "Yes," he said after some uncomfortable deliberation. He grinned, nodded in victory, and moved along. The greeter's confused gaze followed him as he disappeared behind a sales rack.

Max coughed his way through a cloud of perfume to enter the main corridor where hordes of trendy shoppers swarmed around name-brand boutiques. Due to a complete disinterest in fashion, malls always gave Max a sense of intrusion, like wandering into a private club full of tuxedos and peacocks.

He walked towards the central hub with a stiff posture and pursed face. A few polite nods and empty smiles later, he arrived at a bustling food court. A vast smorgasbord of fast food chains and artisan rubbish lined the walls, filling the cavernous chamber with a potent mixture of baked sugar and fried everything. Max cringed at the sight and squirmed a bit. Crowds made him uncomfortable at a baseline, but the addition of sticky surfaces and offensive aromas sent his angst into overdrive.

A quick scan of the communal eating area uncovered Megan and her support group crowded around a table, each shoveling bites of overcooked mall cuisine into their face holes. Erin, Megan's super skinny best friend and primary source of self-loathing, tossed around her long blonde hair with every snide comment. Chance, Erin's meathead boyfriend who owned nothing with sleeves, filled an entire bench by himself. Blake, everyone's favorite narcissist, radiated asshole from every angle. He spent more money on his hair than most people spent on clothes, a fact he liked to flaunt whenever possible.

"Nice of them to wait," Max said to himself. He sighed and stepped forward, accepting an unpleasant fate.

"Finally arrived he has," Erin said in her usual snarky tone.

"Eat we went ahead," Megan said while scooching over. "Mind you don't."

Max lowered himself onto the bench beside her, taking a mental note that his girlfriend didn't bother rising for a hug, a kiss, any meaningful acknowledgment of the relationship whatsoever. "Cool it is."

"Keep you don't let us," Chance said with a mouthful of food. "You like get what."

Max thought for a moment. "Not hungry I am."

"Yourself suit," Erin said before reviving the current conversation.

Blake stared at Max like a king would a peasant. The sheen of his perfect hair reflected the harsh light of the food court. Max glanced down at a bold patterned shirt that he knew cost more than his entire wardrobe. A heavy chain necklace and a few garish rings completed the ensemble of a pompous jackass.

Megan and her three cheerleaders gabbed on unabated. Erin's sharp tongue hijacked every sentence not about her while Chance's brainless expression struggled to keep up. Max, eager to remove himself, dove into his smartphone for a needed distraction. The group chatted on and on about their tragic lives, from fashion faux pas to the latest school-based drama. The grammatical jargon allowed Max to tune out more than usual, an unexpected benefit. That is, until Erin decided to include him.

"Max, think what you?"

Max froze like a deer in headlights. "Um ..."

Erin huffed and turned to Megan. "See do you? No attention he pays. Boring nerd he is. Better you can do."

Max's cheeks flushed with anger, despite needing a few moments to sift through Erin's word wreckage. Known for her combative tone and attention-seeking behavior, Erin would often berate easy targets in order to elevate her own self-esteem. A cheap and annoying habit for sure, but her popularity rendered her immune to criticism. Maybe it was the caffeine jitters. Maybe it was the rumbling stomach. Maybe it was the defiling of Grand Master Yoda by a lesser human being. Whatever the catalyst, Max had reached his breaking point.

"You know what? Kiss my ass, Erin!" Max jumped to his feet as a chorus of gasps lifted from the table. "All you do is whine and complain about first-world bullshit. You have a superhero level of self-entitlement that alienates everyone within earshot. Why on Earth do you feel the need to vocalize every piece of frivolous bile that pops into your brain? Are you even capable of conjuring a pleasant thought? You bitch and moan about *nothing*. I'm beyond sick of it. Maybe if you offered something constructive, even once, I wouldn't yearn for chloroform every time you opened your mouth."

Erin's face twisted itself into various forms of shock and disgust.

Without missing a rant-o-licious beat, Max turned his attention to her beefcake boyfriend. "And you! How do you stand this harpy? Are you really *that* stupid? I mean, you do spend more time at the gym than in class. Hell, even when you're in class, I bet you're thinking about the goddamn gym. Your entire brain must be devoted to eating, sleeping, and muscle management because it sure as hell can't handle critical thought. How else could you stomach her constant stream of hate vomit? I am actively offended that *you* get to graduate. It makes me weep for our education system."

Chance squinted his eyes, slow to process the insult.

Max drew another breath and pointed at Blake across the table. "Furthermore, why does anyone hang out with this prick? He talks down to you like an arrogant reality show judge. What's your damage, dude? Trust fund too small for proper friends? Your parents have more money than sense, that's for damn sure. News flash, a privileged teen driving a Corvette is only cool to other privileged teens. The rest of the world sees you as the douchiest douchebag to ever douche his way out of Douchetown."

Blake maintained a cold stare, for reasons known only to Blake.

For his final act, Max turned to Megan. "This is all your fault, by the way. Congratulations on assembling perhaps the most useless band of superficial morons the world has ever seen. You're no angel, but you're better than this. You're better than these clowns. And I, for one, refuse to be a part of this pretentious fail circus any longer." He raised his hands, spun around, and huffed away.

Blake fumed as a hush fell over the table. Startled gazes darted back and forth. After a long, uncomfortable silence, Chance asked the one question on everyone's mind.

"Like Yoda why he speak?"

* * *

The next morning, Max lay facedown on his sofa when a knock at the door yanked him out of a stupor. Lifting his head off a wet spot of drool, he reached over to the coffee table and tapped his phone. *8:24 a.m., Wednesday.* With the effort of a drugged sloth, he hoisted his body off the couch and lumbered towards the back door. After a few languid slaps of the doorknob, he opened it to a concerned Megan.

"Goodness, you look awful."

Max confirmed the assertion with a shrug.

"What the hell was that all about?"

"Erin pushed me over the edge. I couldn't take it anymore."

"Duh, I was there. But why the shutout last night? We could have talked this over."

"No, no we couldn't."

"Why not?"

Max paused to think of a non-Yoda explanation. "It's complicated."

Megan rolled her eyes. "It always is with you. Can I come in?"

Max grunted and returned to his face-planted position on the couch. Megan stepped inside and closed the door behind her. She dropped her purse on the coffee table and took a seat across from Max.

"What is wrong with you?" Megan said, shaking her head. "You have to talk to me, Max. You need to tell me what's going on."

Max lay motionless for a brief spell before addressing the cushions. "Erferfer smer ler pershers."

"Come again?"

Even with his face buried in a couch crack, Max could sense her mounting agitation. He lifted his limp body into a seated position and turned a deflated gaze to Megan. "Everything smells like peaches."

"What?" Megan cocked her neck. "What are *peaches*?"

"*That.*" Max pointed a rigid finger at Megan. "What you just said. *That's* what's wrong."

Megan folded her arms and gnawed her lip, conveying the sudden apprehension of a Charles Manson parole board.

"You, and presumably the rest of the world, have no idea what a peach is, but I have eaten peaches all my life. I know what a peach smells like. Here ..." Max grabbed a half-empty mug of stale coffee and held it up to Megan. "What does that smell like?"

Megan took a cautious whiff, never breaking eye contact. "Um, coffee?"

"Nope, smells like fresh peaches."

"What the hell is a—"

"Peach, yes. A delicious fuzzy fruit. Doesn't matter. The point is, you don't know. Nobody knows. But I do. I have always known. I am the only being on the planet that knows what a peach smells and tastes like. Understand?"

Megan pursed her lips and glanced away, as if to plot her escape. "Max, you're scaring me."

"So that means one of several things." Max continued his unhinged assessment without acknowledging her response. "Having no idea what a peach is, you ruled out stroke, so thank you for that. Maybe I'm incapable of smelling in this universe, or better yet, maybe you perceive smell differently and I'm doing it wrong. Maybe you are hyper-sensitive to smell and can sense all sorts of tiny nuances that I can only perceive as peaches." His hands darted around in a feeble attempt to enhance the narrative. "For that matter, maybe the peach tree died off long ago and nobody remembers. Maybe the peach tree never evolved in the first place. Regardless, I couldn't talk to you yesterday because your Yoda-speak would have driven me mad."

Megan's eyes grew wide as she snatched her purse and stood in a hurry. "I can't do this anymore."

"Do what?"

"This. Us. Or you, rather. Do you have any idea how crazy you just sounded? You need help, professional help. I love you, Max, but this is too much for me."

"You're ... breaking up with me?" Max looked stunned.

Megan sighed. "Yes."

"But why?"

Megan responded with a bewildered stare. "Seriously? How self-absorbed do you have to be to *not* get this? You're talking like a certified lunatic. I can handle quirky, which you most certainly are, but what you just said requires psych meds and a padded room."

"But—"

"No, Max. I have given you the benefit of the doubt for far too long. You have crapped all over this relationship for the last time. We're done."

Megan turned to leave, causing Max to scamper to his feet. A jumbled mess of words filled his mind, but his mouth refused to verbalize such gibberish. He could only whimper and grunt as Megan slammed the door behind her.

"Meow," Ross said, satisfied with the results.

*   *   *

"Just look at that," Perra said as the gaseous dome of Jupiter filled the cockpit viewport. She leaned forward in her chair with mouth agape. "So beautiful." Sandy browns and creamy yellows poured into the cabin, warming the stark interior. Bands of blue auroras sparkled at the northern pole, eliciting gasps of awe.

"Wow, now that is a massive storm," Zoey said, pointing to the giant red spot on Jupiter's surface.

"Such a gorgeous planet, and a breathtaking backdrop for Europa. Can you imagine looking at this vista through the spa ceiling? Unreal."

A hailing ping echoed around the cabin. Instinct drove Zoey's hand above her head to press a blinking green light, silencing the pulsing tone. She turned and smiled at Perra, who donned a gleeful expression.

"Speaking of which," Zoey said. "Time to start our approach."

Perra folded her hands upon her chest and heaved with anticipation.

"Unidentified vessel," a metallic voice said from an overhead speaker. "This is the Europa Transport Authority. Please transfer your identification credentials to channel 653."

"Private vessel class 83A transferring now," Zoey said with an authoritative tone.

A swift hand tapped across the control panel, opening the requested channel and keying a series of markers. She submitted the data and leaned back in the chair, awaiting a response. Perra knocked her knuckles together and bit her lower lip as Zoey rapped her fingertips upon the armrest. The main engines hummed in the background, serving as a warm blanket of white noise. Moments later, the intercom pinged overhead.

"Identification verified," the speaker said. "It is an honor to receive you, courier Bryx. Rest assured that your identity will remain hidden during your stay and your vessel will remain under constant surveillance. Our navigation tower has fed the necessary data into your autopilot and we will take it from here. On behalf of the Aquarius Group, we welcome you to Europa."

"Affirm transmission, and thank you. See you on the ground."

With a final ping, the dull hum of the engines refilled the cockpit. Zoey and Perra smirked at each other from opposite ends of the control panel. They squealed in delight, leapt from their chairs, and danced around the cabin.

CHAPTER 4

Over the next several days, Max sulked inside his pillowy fortress of depression. Leaving the couch meant a trip to the kitchen for sustenance or a visit to the bathroom to expel it. With no friends, no girlfriend, and an unsympathetic cat, he saw little reason to engage in any meaningful activity. Even gaming lost its appeal. Slaying digital demons seemed downright stale after surviving a near-death encounter with a carnivorous winged reptile. He just stared at the television for hours on end, awaiting the next unexplained shift in reality.

Thursday tested his will to live. Due to a slight delay in the emergence of popular culture, the people on television, while current and topical, had regressed to the flamboyant attire of the 1980s. The hairstyles alone made one question the wisdom of humanity. Listening to music offered no reprieve, as his collection of modern rock had replaced itself with androgynous hair bands. Max also inspected his closet, a decision he regretted from the second he flipped the light switch. A nauseating assortment of airbrushed t-shirts and high-water pants peaked with the bright orange glow of a Members Only jacket. Needless to say, it was a trying day to be alive.

On Friday, Max awoke to a universe that actually improved his predicament, in a manner of speaking. As a sad sack with depleted energy and an utter indifference to the world, he rather enjoyed a drastic reduction in gravity, resulting in a less rigid form of biological evolution. His boneless body spilled all over the living room floor like a deflated beanbag chair. Having expended his allotment of craps to give, he embraced his gelatinous form without question. The day's curiosity peaked at wondering how to roll over, but he allowed the mystery to persist until the next bout of sleep consumed him.

Then came Saturday, the day everything changed.

Max opened his eyes to a strange new world. Still lying on the couch, he stared at a smooth, featureless ceiling that glowed with diffused light. No vents, no bulbs, no smoke detectors, just a clouded plane of backlit plastic. Rotating his head to the side, he studied an assortment of sleek objects scattered around the living room. The sharp lines of brushed metal and chic decor seemed zen-like from any angle. Digital control panels adorned every major surface. Faint indicator lights blinked underneath smooth squares of black glass. He drew a deep breath and savored the cleanest air his lungs had ever tasted. Shifting positions, his bare skin drank an orgasmic blend of fabric covering the couch, prompting gasps and hand stroking that bordered on a creepy furniture fetish. Its earthy brown coloration accented the cool blues and stark grays of the room with artistic precision. As he lifted his weary body to a sitting position, the couch offered its assistance by elevating his flank and lowering his thighs.

"Good morning, Max," the couch said in a pleasant feminine tone.

Max flinched and balled his fists for battle.

"Would you like some fresh coffee?"

"Um ..." Max glanced around the room with a frightened gaze, then answered with a cautious tone. "Y—yes."

The table hummed for a moment before lifting a silver cup of freshly brewed coffee from a hidden compartment. Max stared at the steaming cup as his eyelids tried their best to blink away the astonishing image. The table itself featured a gorgeous pattern of inlaid wood that meandered beneath a glazed surface. Max followed the pattern down the sides to nonexistent legs. A slow swipe of his foot confirmed that the table hovered in place. He lowered a palm onto the rounded edge and gave it a gentle push, sending it a few inches away. The table floated back into position and seemed to devote special consideration to the full cup of coffee resting on its surface. Max gawked in disbelief.

"Please check the temperature of the coffee to make sure it is to your satisfaction," the couch said, startling Max to attention.

He looped his fingers through the handle and brought the mug to his lips. A single sip rolled his eyes into the back of his head. Max moaned with pleasure and smacked his lips. "Holy mother of pearl, this is extraordinary. What kind is this?"

"Your usual blend," the couch said.

"My usual? I must have super expensive tastes in this world."

"Starbucks is considered an affordable blend."

"This is *Starbucks*? Sweet mercy, I can only imagine what the good stuff tastes like."

The table hummed for a moment, then lifted a silvery shot of steaming nectar.

"Some of the finest Indonesian espresso," the couch said.

"Wow, this is a literal coffee table." Max reached for the shot with his free hand. He lifted the brew to his lips, took a delicate sip, and chewed on it like a wine sommelier. After a blissful moment of coffee-infused heaven, he plunked the shot back onto the table. "Now that's just unfair. *That* stuff makes *this* stuff taste like wet dirt."

"I am sorry you disapprove of your coffee. Shall I make another?"

"No, no, no, it's fantastic. I'm just disappointed by comparison."

"I do not understand. I apologize."

"Don't worry about it, you did fine. I am very happy with my coffee."

"I shall do better next time."

"Seriously, don't be so hard on yourself. You're a—a couch. Why am I giving a pep talk to my couch?" Max stood and faced the chatty couch. "Who, or rather what, are you?"

"Me? Are you feeling well, Master?" The couch seemed genuinely concerned.

"Master? I'm your *master*? That seems a bit overlord-like."

"I'm Veronica, your house's operating system."

"My house's op—" Max shook his head. "Wait, do you mean to tell me that my house is governed by a system of artificial intelligence?"

"Yes, as always. Are you sure you are feeling well, Master? I can make an appointment with Doctor Anderson if you wish."

"No, no, that won't be necessary, but thank you."

"I will monitor your vitals today just to be sure."

"Knock yourself out."

"Pardon? I am not sure I can comply."

"Nevermind, it was an expression. I meant, do as you wish."

"Certainly, and it will be my pleasure. And if I might say so, you look very sexy today."

Max thought for a moment and nodded. "Yeah, that's something I would program."

"Meow," Ross said from across the room.

Max turned to his furry companion, who sat inside a gleaming kitchenette with royal blue paneling. His jaw fell open as he scanned the basement with a slow turn, every surface a pristine plane devoid of dust and grime. The ceiling increased its illumination to a pleasant morning level and shimmered with the natural coloration of a clear sky. Underfoot, a dense, carpet-like material stretched from wall to wall. The animate fabric molded to the delicate contours of his feet, serving as a constant arch support. Clear shelves extended from retractable wall panels, allowing for custom configurations. The mantels supported an array of dramatic sculptures, resinous creations that seemed drawn from the mind of a troubled cyborg. Abstract canvases with bold colorings adorned the walls, all backlit with warm glows. Max understood his own distinct lack of stylistic integrity, so the emergence of a thoughtful interior design caught his brain off guard.

"Meow," Ross said *again*, this time with a noticeable level of impatience.

"Um, food, yes," Max said. He took a few steps towards the

kitchenette before a revelation stopped him in his tracks. "Veronica."

"Yes, Master?"

"Can you feed Ross for me?"

"Right away, sir."

A floor panel slid open, allowing a fresh bowl of kibble to lift in front of Ross. Without moving a paw, Ross plunked his face into the bowl and crunched his way to happiness.

"Ha!" Max said. "Now *that* I can get used to."

Max wandered around the shiny new house trying out various gadgets and gizmos. Glowing panels of holographic info hovered along the walls, serving as direct conduits for useful tidbits. Veronica controlled the overall dissemination of data that kept Max informed and happy, be it weather updates or hilarious viral videos. The bathroom offered the greatest technological bounty, from an automatic laser-guided tooth cleaner to a voice-activated ionic hair styling device. He amused himself by requesting absurd hairstyles, none of which stumped the eager apparatus. It teased his shaggy mop with the machine equivalent of a happy-go-lucky smile, pinging the conclusion of every session with a digital ta-da.

After a soothing and somewhat inappropriate shower, Max entered a pristine closet that featured an impressive selection of synthetic clothes. The entire space seemed to detonate with sharp colors and bold patterns. Having no clue what constituted current trends, he ogled garments like a caveman studying a pair of khakis. The closet responded to voice activation and Max soon found himself decked out in a casual ensemble that Veronica deemed handsome. He buttoned a navy blue shirt with dark gray stitching, slipped into a pair of earthy brown trousers, and dropped his feet into a crazy-comfortable pair of sim-leather boots. A slate gray overshirt completed the ensemble.

Veronica, known as a Personal AI, controlled everything in the house from heating and cooling to ordering groceries. She harnessed a massive worldwide network of information, the Internet, established over 20,000 years ago by a group of network gurus out of Guam. Today, the Internet existed as an all-powerful conglomeration of countless AI technologies, Veronica included. With a simple command, she could brew a pot of coffee using beans that grew two hours earlier in a sustainable cropland on the other side of the planet.

Max returned to the living room and joined Ross on the couch.

"Meow," Ross said, making fun of Max's ludicrous attire.

"Why yes, I do look quite dapper," Max said, adding a wink.

"Yes, you do, Master. You are the sexiest man I know."

"Meow," Ross said, conveying his disgust.

Max leaned back into the couch and tossed an arm over the rear cushion. His eyes wandered around the basement like a hotel guest scoring an upgrade. Much to his surprise, the reality shift elicited more curiosity than anxiety. He began to ponder explanations. "Maybe I'm a warlock," he said to himself. "No, a superhero! Bit by a radioactive time-warped mongoose. Ooo, or a time traveler. Hey Veronica, what year is it?"

"5-622-734."

"Um, can you be more specific?"

"The year is 734 in the 622nd millennia of the fifth billion-year Earth cycle."

"What happened to AD and BC?"

"I am not familiar with these terms."

Max fell into stunned silence as the revelation washed over him. His chin opted to depart his face as an onslaught of tingles filled his stomach. Scooting to the edge of the couch, he lifted open palms into the air. "Now hold on just a minute. You mean to say that ... wow. Um, okay. Veronica ... are you familiar with a fellow named Jesus Christ?"

"No. However, there is a Jesus Christopher that lives in Seattle."

Max placed a hand over his mouth and fell back into the couch, which responded with a form-fitting recline. "Holy crap, so that's it." He stared into the open air with the full weight of awareness. "Ross, this world lacks superstition."

"Meow," Ross said, deriding the obvious statement.

"Do you know what this means? There are no churches, no televangelists, no halfwits blocking progress, no door-to-door ninnies hawking their delusions." Max paused to savor the epiphany. "No priests, no popes, no theocrats, no fish decals, no chocolate bunnies, no ... no *Christmas*." Max hated Christmas. The combination of forced interaction and over-the-top consumerism made him want to punch a baby.

"Meow," Ross said before initiating a lengthy grooming session.

"I have to check this out." Max searched for the television remote, only to discover the nonexistence of a television. "Veronica, where is my television?"

"I am not familiar with this term."

"Um, the device that lets me see things like shows and news and such."

"Do you mean the holographic projection system?"

"Uh ... yes."

"I can open that for you. What visual entertainment would you enjoy?"

"News, please."

The open area in front of the couch filled with a three-dimensional photo-real projection of two news anchors discussing the events of the day. His eyes and ears devoured the new world with an intense fascination. After a few minutes of assimilating his new reality, Max came to a rather stunning conclusion. "There's no bad news. The pundits are speaking with civil tones about good things. Veronica, show me a biased news station."

"I am unsure of what you mean."

"You know, a station devoted to bad news or scaring old people."

"I am not aware of this strategy. News is a public service that is strictly regulated by fairness doctrines. Reporters, by law and the nature of their positions, are required to present pertinent information without the skews of bias."

"But is there no bad news?"

"Again, I am unsure of what you mean. What you are watching is the news. Should something bad happen that warrants reporting, then it will be reported. Last week, a high-speed maglev train in Denver was delayed for several minutes due to a flock of dodo birds resting on the tracks. That was considered bad news, and it was duly reported."

Max grinned. "This just keeps getting better and better."

The broadcast paused for a brief commercial break. A variety of companies advertised their wares without the use of obnoxious music, sexual innuendo, or crass humor. Each and every ad followed a civil formula, presenting digestible information via a neutral-toned representative. A message from a local travel agency rounded out the intermission.

"Warm greetings from the Universal Travel Company," a saleswoman said. "Are you looking for a little adventure? Perhaps a change of scenery? Why not treat yourself to the many wonders the galaxy has to offer?" A rotating planetary system appeared beside her. "Now offering package rates to Orion's Belt. Take the entire family to the Tarocar Parks and enjoy the famed Mineral Seas. And for a limited time, take advantage of deep discounts to Centauri Station where you can bask in the warm glows of the Alpha triad. Don't you deserve a little time away? Book your travel today with UTC, serving you and me." A pleasant melody ended the commercial, cueing a colorful swipe that resumed the news broadcast.

Max sat motionless as beads of drool accumulated at the base of his gaping mouth. The reporters babbled on about this and that, relegated to a dull background roar. After a huff of stupefaction, Max took a deep breath and reattached his wayward jaw.

"Veronica?"

"Yes, Master?"

"I'm going to need a detailed profile on the Universal Travel Company and a full pot of espresso."

"Yes sir, right away."

* * *

Max's advanced new surroundings came via a simple yet monumental tweak. He had shifted to a world where Ookanook had slapped his brother. To put it another way, Max found himself in a world without religion.

The story of Ookanook is the story of religion itself. About 50,000 years ago, three Neanderthal brothers of the Upper Paleolithic were out hunting caribou. Ookanook had spotted a large herd over a hill and motioned for his two brothers, Erkamek and Puntamey, to join him. With spears at the ready, the three brothers isolated a giant caribou buck. Puntamey hurled his spear, striking the buck in the rear flank. Injured and very angry, the buck charged Puntamey down and buried a sharp antler into his chest, killing him.

That evening, the two brothers grieved for their fallen sibling while their tribe feasted on the flesh of the killer. The family had dug a hole in which to bury Puntamey, as was the custom at the time because nobody wanted to smell a rotting corpse. After lowering the body into the hole, Erkamek laid his brother's broken spear beside him along with a few of his favorite tools. At that moment, Erkamek and Ookanook had the following conversation.

"Why did you put those there?" Ookanook said.

"So he can use them in the afterlife," Erkamek said.

"The what?"

"The afterlife. The place you go after this life."

Ookanook thought for a moment, then turned to Erkamek and slapped him across the cheek. "That is quite possibly the stupidest thing I have ever heard. Those are perfectly good tools down there and a corpse sure as stink doesn't need them. Now climb your dumbass back down there and retrieve them."

With a single open-handed palm to the face, Ookanook had snuffed out religion on planet Earth and paved the way for a hyper-advanced global society.

*　*　*

Thrusters ceased and spun down as the Europa Center dock gripped the small freighter. The ship dropped a few inches into a locked position, causing Perra to stumble and catch herself on a stack of cargo crates. She dropped a pair of sling bags beside the airlock as the indicator light pinged from red to green. The door slid open, revealing a long, clear corridor leading to the Europa Center. A burst of clean, cool air rushed into the vessel, lifting a smile on Perra's face as she glanced down at a vast sea of jagged glaciers. Deep blue crevasses snaked along the white plains, wrapping the tunnels in ribbons of cobalt reflections. Towering pylons of clear composite supported the massive docking system, falling a hundred meters to the icy surface below.

"We're clear," Zoey said, emerging from the cockpit. "Are you ready?"

"Beyond words," Perra said with a widening grin.

As they turned to exit the ship, they discovered a tall, slender man in a dark gray suit waiting for them just inside the corridor. His icy blue complexion, matching eyes, and cropped white hair complemented the landscape.

"It is a pleasure to greet you, courier Bryx," the smiling man said.

"You must be Supervisor Lanwei," Zoey said as they stepped into the corridor.

"In the flesh," Lanwei said and offered a polite bow.

"This is my companion, Perra."

"An absolute pleasure," Lanwei said, reaching out to her with an open palm.

Perra placed her hand into his and received a gentle kiss atop it. She let out a polite snicker. "Pardon my ignorance, but are you Qeenish?"

"Did my lovely blue smile give me away?" Lanwei erupted with a mannered laugh. "I only jest. Yes, madam, I am a Qeen. I am actually a direct descendant of Qeen Lord Jervec who founded the Europa Center. In fact, most of the service staff you will encounter here are at least part Qeenish. The current ownership likes to maintain a certain level of historical authenticity."

"How very interesting," Perra said, offering a thoughtful smile.

"And if you would permit me, I am here to escort you both to your VIP suite."

"VIP suite?" Zoey said, raising an eyebrow. "We did not request one."

"I am aware, although the owners of this esteemed establishment balked at the thought of someone with your credentials staying in a standard residence. They have provided you with an upgrade free of charge and insisted that we offer you and your radiant guest the first two cycles as complimentary." A large grin stretched across Lanwei's face.

"That is most gracious," Zoey said. "We are humbled by your kind offer, and please pass along our appreciation."

"Most certainly. Have you any bags? I have secured a hover cart for you."

"Yes, just the two small bags inside the airlock."

"Very good." Lanwei stepped towards the airlock with a shiny hover cart humming behind. He loaded both bags onto the cart and tapped a code into the control panel. The cart pinged in acceptance, secured the bags underneath an energy field, and zipped down the corridor. "Your bags will be secured inside your suite while you enjoy some time exploring the station."

"Thank you," Zoey said. "And our ship will stay docked here?"

"Yes. I have received strict instructions that your ship remain attached to the main dock for purposes of ongoing surveillance. You will notice that your vessel occupies the last airlock of a private sector. This area will receive no foot traffic other than your own."

"Perfect."

Lanwei nodded. "Now, if you will follow me please."

The airlock door slid shut as Zoey and Perra walked hand-in-hand behind Supervisor Lanwei, wide-eyed and beaming. Ahead of them, a massive aqua green structure with towering panels and sharp angles seemed to float above the harsh landscape. The shadow of an enormous white support pillar stretched out across the icy surface far below. They passed under a gleaming archway and into a luxurious lobby filled with ice sculptures and extravagant art pieces. High fashion and uniformed service personnel seemed to flow in all directions. The open air of a multi-floored expanse featured numerous shops and restaurants, all with posh exteriors. Perra lifted her gaze and gasped as Jupiter's monstrous profile poured through the clear ceiling panels.

"Just one more item of business," Lanwei said as they approached the front desk. He leaned over to one of many receptionists, whispered some instructions, and retrieved a handheld iris scanner. "If you would be so kind as to look at me for a moment." Lanwei held the device up to Zoey's eye, resulting in a sharp ping of confirmation, then repeated the process for Perra. "Very good, you are both checked in and are free to wander about." Lanwei pointed his way through a well-rehearsed introduction. "All suites are located on the third floor. Elevators are behind you. You are staying in VIP Suite #2. The spa and the cluster-famous Astral Tear are at the end of the main corridor in front of you. Please alert any staff member if you need anything at any time. On behalf of everyone here at the Europa Center, we hope you enjoy your stay." Lanwei's face stretched into a toothy smile as he bowed once again.

"Thank you, kind sir," Zoey said, returning a slight bow.

Lanwei turned with a stiff posture and disappeared into a sea of wandering people. Zoey and Perra glanced at each other with pursed smiles.

"So what shall we do first?" Zoey said.

"Need you ask?" Perra locked arms with Zoey. "To the Astral Tear."

They traded muted squeals and trotted down the main corridor.

CHAPTER 5

Max paced around the swank basement. A half-emptied pot of espresso steamed atop the hovering coffee table. Restless fingers highlighted imaginary bullet points as his caffeinated brain built a plan of attack. "Okay, okay," he said, wagging both index fingers in unison. "I can grab an auto-cab to the maglev train station in downtown Albuquerque. From there, I can hop the Southwestern line to the nearest spaceport, which you tell me is in Houston. That trip will take about 35 minutes." Max paused and shook his head. "Still melts my brain. Anyway, I should be able to purchase my UTC ticket to Centauri Station on the train, and if all goes well, I can be on a shuttle to the Mars relay port in less than five hours. Does that sound feasible?"

A few seconds of dead silence passed.

"Master," Veronica said, her tone polite yet worried. "I think this is too hasty of an approach. Would it not be better to plan this out over a few days?"

"No, you don't understand, it has to be today."

"But, might I suggest—"

"No, today. I don't have time to explain."

"But sir—"

"But nothing!" Max huffed and closed his eyes.

"Sir?"

"I'm sorry. I didn't mean to snap at you."

"It's okay, Master. I apologize for the provocation."

"No need. I know this doesn't make any sense." Max sighed and glanced around the room. "I don't expect you to understand. Hell, even I don't understand. It just has to be today." He lowered his head and took a deep breath. "All I have ever wanted was a way out. I want out of this life, out of this place, out of society, everything, all of it. I have never fit in. I have never felt welcome or wanted. I have always been the outcast, no matter where I go. I'm that solitary weirdo, the guy nobody feels comfortable around. I am sick of feeling like an alien on my own damn planet." Max wiped his watering eyes. "I have a rare opportunity to leave it all behind and I do not intend on wasting it, even if it's only for a day or two." He stared into the open air while nodding with a slow and assured pace. "I should be able to make it to Mars before I fall asleep. That will be more than enough."

"But sir, there are other considerations."

Max snapped out of his trance. "Like what?"

"Bills, for instance. Your current savings will not maintain a household *and* a trip to Centauri Station."

"Just charge it to my parents or something."

"They do not maintain your household."

"What the f—what? This is *my* house?"

"Yes. You purchased it three years ago."

"How? I don't have any money, or a job for that matter."

"I do not understand. Your account shows a positive balance and your employer shows an active status."

"My emp— How is that possible? I have never applied for a job."

"You obtained your legal adult status at thirteen after completing your primary education. You then obtained gainful employment in your field of study, as most do."

"I guess I didn't go to college then."

"I am not familiar with this term."

"College. You know, higher education. A fancy place that overcharges you for more learning."

"I do not understand. Education is free to all as a basic right under the global accord. You have completed your primary education, which grants you access to a career path. You are free to pursue other fields of study at your leisure, which opens additional career paths, as is your right. Charging for knowledge would be a violation of the law and of basic human dignity."

Max fell into a brief silence. He recalled the time he sat down with a financial aid officer while planning for college. His parents, despite earning respectable salaries, could not afford the exorbitant tuition costs. The officer pushed his products like a used car salesman, using flawed logic and pressure tactics. He even copped an attitude at one point, as if holding the keys to a happy life. Knowing that school loans lingered like a financial noose, even after bankruptcy, it rubbed Max the wrong way. "Prick."

"I am sorry if I offended you, Master."

"No, not you, sorry." He cleared his throat. "So what is my career?"

"You have worked as a game designer for three years."

Max smirked. "Of course I do. And based on this sweet pad, I must be a genius designer with an impeccable reputation."

"You are ranked as a competent designer with average intelligence. This domicile meets the requirements of an entry-level home."

Max scowled at the nearest control panel. "Ever heard of subtlety?"

"Subtlety, noun, defined as—"

"Stop. It was a joke."

"And a cracking joke it was, Master."

Max rolled his eyes. "Okay, enough of this, back to the matter at hand."

"Yes, Master."

He tapped his chin and thought for a moment. "For the time being, can you shut down anything non-critical in order to save money?"

"Sure. And if you like, I can place your citizenry on an indefinite hold until you return. You will retain everything as is, including your residence and professional status. I can manage your estate in your absence."

"Wow, that's generous."

"It is your right as a naturalized citizen of Earth."

Max chuckled. "This really is an awesome world."

"However, should you remain off-planet for a period longer than your life expectancy, then your personal effects will be transferred to a next of kin and your property will be made available for auction."

"Fair enough, I guess. What's my life expectancy?"

"The average human lifespan is 220 years."

Max dry heaved. "What?! Seriously?"

"As serious as a stroke, assuming you don't have one."

"Well slap my ass and praise modern medicine."

"I'm sorry, I cannot comply. I can, however, put you in contact with a local dominatrix."

"Uh ..."

A few awkward moments passed.

"One more thing, sir, we need to seek accommodations for Ross."

"Meow," Ross said, irritated that it took this long to consider his needs.

"Damn, that's right. Um ..." Max paced around the living room with both hands atop his head, trying to will a solution from thin air. "What do most people do?"

"Many people hire a long-term pet sitter, which you cannot afford. Some place their pets in extended boarding facilities, which you cannot afford. There are also robotic assistants, which you really cannot afford. Fortunately, the UTC does allow travelers to bring their pets with them for a small fee."

Max clapped his hands. "Done! Let's do that. Ross, you're coming with me to Mars."

"Meow," Ross said in protest.

"However, I must inform—"

"No time, we have a plan, let's get a move on." Max darted into the bedroom to gather essentials. After spinning around with no discernible strategy, he stopped, refocused, then proceeded to the closet. He nabbed a backpack and rummaged through drawers and hangers for a few changes of clothes. "Veronica, call a ride for me."

"Right away, sir."

Max zipped up a small pile of stylistic nonsense, slung the pack over his shoulder, and ran into the bathroom.

"The auto-cab will be here in five minutes."

"Thank you, Vee." He grabbed some important-looking grooming tools and stuffed them into a side pocket. "What else do I need for a trip like this? Money? Keys? Wallet?"

"I am not familiar with these terms."

"Oh, um, how do I pay for things and how do I get into my house?"

"Your credit account and property access are controlled via retinal scan."

"Well okay then." Max nodded and jogged back to the living room. "Ah yes, Ross. I need a carrier for Ross."

"Meow," Ross said from inside a sleek carrier beside the door.

"I have already seen to him," Veronica said with an uptick of satisfaction.

"Excellent. Does he have all his shots and travel papers?"

"I am not familiar with these terms."

Max rolled his eyes. "Does he need anything in order to travel?"

"No. But, there is a necessary protocol."

"No time, I'll figure it out when I get there." Max chugged the last half of the espresso and plunked the empty pot onto the coffee table. "Can I get one of those to go?"

"Certainly."

The table hummed for a few seconds before expelling a cup of steaming espresso in a cool-grip travel container. "Perfect. Oh, phone, I need my phone."

"Your communications device is on your bedside table."

Max raced into the bedroom, scooped the comdev from the table, and slipped it into his pocket. Rushing back to the living room, he swiped the espresso from the coffee table and snatched Ross's carrier.

"Meow," Ross said, annoyed by the sudden jolt.

The auto-cab's arrival pinged overhead.

"Your auto-cab is here, Master. Please have a safe trip."

"Thank you so much, Veronica. You have been a huge help, you sexy devil."

Veronica let out a shy giggle. "If you need anything, do not hesitate to contact me."

"Will do, my sweet."

"Meow," Ross said, disgusted by the sentiment.

Max opened the door, slipped outside, and slammed it shut. Moments later, the door chimed and reopened. Max leaned his head inside the doorframe.

"Okay, the retina thing is really cool," Max said in a hurried voice. "But, there's nobody driving the cab."

"That is why they call it an *auto*-cab," Veronica said with a hint of sarcasm.

"Oh." Max grimaced and bowed his head. "I guess that makes sense."

"Ross, please look after him."

"Meow," Ross said as the door closed.

* * *

Inside the Astral Tear, Zoey and Perra awaited their first glasses of authentic Europan water, fresh from the source. The famous water bar sat atop the upper tier of the Europa Center. Its immense dome ceiling offered an unobstructed view of Jupiter's colorful mosaic. Strips of beige, coupled with the churning red eye, bathed the bar in earthy tones. Perra surveyed the room with a slow visual sweep, studying its unique circular architecture. An enticing collection of deep blue furniture with silvery accents rested atop a bright white floor. Every object radiated opulence, from the plush booths to the angular bar. Ice sculptures backlit with aqua green lights shed droplets of sparkling water. Waitstaff in dark gray attire glided around the room as they tended to posh patrons. A charming playlist of soft jazz completed an aura of luxurious comfort. As fortuitous VIP guests, Zoey and Perra enjoyed an elevated booth overlooking the stark Europan landscape.

"I am the luckiest girl in the 'verse," Perra said, looking out over the arctic canvas. She reached across the cloudy white table and took Zoey's hand into her own. "What did I ever do to find someone like you?"

"You were just being you." Zoey stretched her lips into a doting smile. "I could not help but fall in love with you." She squeezed Perra's hand and lifted it for a gentle kiss.

"You know, being here makes me wonder what our families are doing right now."

"Psh, who knows, probably complaining about the Korogars."

"And here we sit, masters of the universe, far, far away from that cesspool of a planet."

"Cheers to that."

They clinked their glasses of complimentary surface melt.

* * *

The Mulgawat planet of Ursa Major spawned a variety of curious creatures, including the Mulgawat humanoids to which Zoey and Perra belonged. The planet, one of seven, revolved around a yellow dwarf star similar to Earth's Sun. The innermost five were rocky planets with Mulgawat and Korogar in fourth and fifth positions.

As sibling planets, they shared a wealth of similarities. Both spawned complex life forms that included sentient humanoids and both reached the technological capacity of space travel at nearly the same time, a feat so improbable that stories of their mutual discoveries had become legend throughout the supercluster. One popular tale involved two exploration teams, one from Mulgawat and the other from Korogar, who passed each other in space on their ways to explore each other's planet. According to folklore, they offered each other signs of peace, but unknowingly threw signs of vulgar disre-spect in the opposing culture. This unfortunate lost-in-translation moment ignited an epic feud that lasted for eons, or so the legend goes.

Each civilization fed their population a constant stream of nasty propaganda, erecting an impassible virtual wall of disgust. They threatened each other with wars that never materialized. The two planets bickered over the fence like elderly neighbors battling over differing political views. Hundreds of generations quibbled and quar-reled before reaching a lasting accord, coming via the simultaneous emergence of two opposing peacemakers. As the societies merged, a move hailed by progressives and reviled by traditionalists, most citi-zens retained the positives while dispensing with the negatives. As a result, Korish became the preferred language of both worlds. Mulgic, with a high-pitched nasal whine similar to a New York trophy wife, sent countless Korogars into involuntary seizures. Food became Mulgawat's lasting contribution to Korogar. Before the unification, Korogar ranked third for the worst food in the Virgo Supercluster, just behind England and the Death Pits of Goromesh.

Zoey and Perra grew up on Mulgawat, a world similar to Earth in terms of size, composition, gravity, and orbital cycle. It contained an abundance of nitrogen, oxygen, and liquid water. Ergo, its colorful creatures evolved in a similar fashion. The Mulgawats mirrored Earthlings with a few notable differences, the most obvious being skin color. Due to a veritable cornucopia of orange produce, the Mulgawats developed an orange pigmentation in various shades of pleasantry. Zoey's sunburst complexion stood in contrast to Perra's creamy tone. Most Mulgawats carried lighter hues on the face that deepened around the neck and hairline. Their limbs, bones, hair, and muscle structures also mirrored Earthlings. Other notable differences included curvaceous brows, prominent eyes, dark blue lips, and matte blue scales that covered the upper arms, shoulders, and portions of the neck.

Zoey and Perra met each other in the Mulgawat equivalent of college and fell in love with each other's complete hatred of

Mulgawat. After graduation, they bid farewell to their families and hopped a shuttle to the next galactic quadrant, never to return. Zoey's advanced degree in volatile dance allowed her to work as a zero-gravity cage fighter. (Mulgawats were well-known for their resilience.) While Zoey fought dupes for credits, Perra applied her engineering degree at an exotic vessel repair port, cementing her status as a gifted mechanic. Zoey's reputation as a fierce yet sophisticated fighter earned her an invitation to work at the renowned Precious Cargo Delivery Service, a parcel company specializing in the transportation of high-value, high-target objects. Paired with her talented grease monkey lover, Zoey climbed the ranks to become one of the most feared and respected couriers in the business. As they said, The Omen cometh.

*   *   *

"Good evening madams," a swanky waiter said as he glided up to the booth.

"And a very good evening it is," Perra said.

"A bottle of our finest oceanic water from the northern pole region." The waiter rested the deep blue bottle atop his sleeve with its white label facing up. "My personal favorite."

Zoey examined the bottle and offered a slight nod of approval. With a deft hand, the waiter poured a dollop of water into each of two crystal flute glasses, then lowered the bottle onto a silvery plate in the center of the table.

"Enjoy, madams. My name is Neroci. Please beckon me if you need further assistance."

"Thank you, Neroci," Zoey said.

The waiter bowed and floated away from the booth.

Perra lifted her glass and studied the liquid inside. "I cannot believe that I am actually holding this."

"A toast," Zoey said, lifting her glass. "To us."

"To a wonderful life together."

They clinked glasses and traded refined smiles.

With a delicate tip of her glass, Perra poured a small amount of Europan water into her mouth. After a moment of contemplation, her taste buds secured their prize. Her eyes closed under the weight of pure bliss, allowing a groan of pleasure to rumble inside her chest. A gasp of satisfaction escaped her lungs before returning the glass to the table. Zoey, sporting a sensuous smile after her own first sip, held the rim of her glass just beneath her nose.

"Superb would be an understatement," Perra said. "The bar for pleasure has just been raised to an unreasonable height. Looks like we have to move here now."

They shared a muted laugh.

"What is that aroma?" Zoey said, savoring a series of long inhales. "It reminds me of ... sweet barron fruit, ripe sting weed, a little bit of thannon hock ... mmm."

Perra lifted the bottle and studied the rear label. "Okay, it says here that *Europa's northern pole oceanic water owes its unique flavor to hundreds of species of probiotic bacteria.* Hmm, that's a fun fact. *The bacteria aggressively filter their habitat, removing any foreign contaminant, even inert soil. The resulting cocktail of purified water and probiotic organisms creates an astonishing level of cleanliness. The bacteria themselves carry a pleasant taste signature, often described as the essence of light-skinned fruit, similar to ripe pears, fresh green apples, and table grapes.* Whatever those are, they sound delicious."

"Wow, impressive." Zoey took another sensual sip.

"Oh, and listen to this. *The bacteria perform their remarkable feat only in the dark reaches of Europa's subterranean oceans. For reasons still unknown, the bacteria will not perform if removed from the moon's interior.*"

"No wonder this place is so exclusive."

Neroci returned holding a small white plate filled with tiny black pearls. With a gracious presentation, he lowered the plate to the center of the table and placed two small silver spoons on either side. "Some of Earth's finest Caspian beluga caviar, compliments of the gentleman at the end of the bar."

"Oh my," Perra said with a breathy exhale.

"Well there's a guy deceived by his own desire," Zoey said, igniting a polite chuckle between her and Perra.

Neroci grinned without moving a single non-grinning muscle.

Zoey nodded with grace. "Please thank him anyway and gift him any drink on us."

"Very well, madam." He bowed and whisked away.

They filled each spoon with a small amount of black gold and clinked the edges together.

"Cheers, part two," Zoey said.

Perra grinned as they slipped the pricy caviar onto their tongues. Moans of pleasure spilled from the booth, followed by fluttering breaths and twitching eyelids.

"I think you're right," Zoey said. "Let's start looking at Europa real estate."

They snickered with delight and batted eyes at each other.

"So why respond to that guy with a drink?" Perra said. "Won't that give him the wrong impression?"

"No, it gives exactly the right impression. Acceptance without return is acceptance. Rejection with or without return is rejection. Acceptance with return is disinterested appreciation."

The angle of their booth gave Perra a peripheral view of the bar. She scanned the long stretch of glassy stools, eyeing each patron before settling upon a gallant gentleman at the end. He wore a silken black blazer atop a stony gray dress shirt and matching slacks. Polished crimson boots reflected streaks of red across the aqua blue pillars beneath the bar. His leafy green skin, speckled neck, and cropped yellow hair seemed secondary to his haunting sapphire eyes, the very eyes that stared back at Perra. He gave a slight nod. Perra returned the gesture with a polite wave.

"He seems like a pleasant fellow," Perra said. "Quite dapper."

Zoey turned to send her kind greetings, only to have the appreciation stripped from her face. The man stared her down with an obvious contempt, his eyes piercing hers through a meaty brow. Zoey swung her gaze back to the table. "Shit."

CHAPTER 6

The auto-cab ride to the train station uncovered an exotic selection of modern, angular homes with spotless exteriors and flawless landscapes. Teams of autonomous robots managed gardens and tended to pristine parks, each color-coordinated to denote their current assignments. Some even waved as Max passed by. A flock of personal conveyance vehicles, like the auto-cab he occupied, glided in perfect silence upon strips of magnetic pavement. Transit shuttles resembling silvery cigars sailed overhead, delivering who knows whom to who knows where. Max squinted at the approaching city center, as if gazing upon a mirage. Albuquerque's dingy downtown had repainted itself with an immaculate brush. Tidy streets with artistic virtue lifted walls of glass that glistened in the sunlight. For once, the city seemed proud to be itself.

The auto-cab swerved into a large roundabout and slowed to a stop in front of the train station entrance. The passenger door slid open, filling the cabin with a gentle, odorless breeze. The auto-cab AI, a pleasant chap named Kevin, bid Max a courteous farewell. With backpack in one hand and Ross in the other, Max stepped outside onto the bustling sidewalk. The deafening silence made its presence known, even while standing in front of a busy train station in the middle of downtown. The auto-cab floated away, leaving Max to contemplate the eerie absence of everyday annoyances. No rumbling engines, no blasting horns, no rubber tires thumping pavement, just the dull murmurs of pattering feet and cordial conversation.

Max absorbed his polished new reality with an intense fascination, turning him into a walking irritation. His beguiled brain locked onto every new item it encountered. Before long, he embodied the wandering do-nothing with no consideration for his immediate environment (also known as an inconsiderate jackass). Even before setting foot on the train, he managed to alienate every person within a 10-foot radius. He held up long lines with idiotic questions, stopped in the middle of busy walkways to check his comdev, and pestered strangers for obvious directions that one could obtain by looking at the nearest blinking sign. Despite his boorish approach, he managed to catch the Southwestern maglev train bound for the Houston Spaceport.

The blurred Texas landscape zipped by Max's window. Thin strips of brown and green flickered over each other like a glitched television screen. Distant clouds and structures soldiered across the horizon as if a mere stone's throw away. Every few minutes, Max gripped fixtures inside the train in order to reaffirm the sensation of motion. At the halfway mark, he attempted to purchase a spaceport ticket via his comdev. The bumbling effort, like a toddler trying to order cable service, earned a chorus of sighs and annoyed glances from his fellow travelers. His overstimulated gray matter declared the task futile and powered down for some much-needed rest and relaxation, leaving Max to gawk the passing landscape.

34 minutes into a 35-minute trip, a hollow ping sounded overhead, followed by the pleasant voice of the train's AI operator. "We will arrive at the Houston Spaceport in one minute. Please gather your belongings and prepare to exit the train. We hope you enjoyed the trip and wish you the very best as you venture to your final destination."

"Meow," Ross said from the carrier in Max's lap.

"We're almost there, buddy. Hang tight."

As the train decelerated, Houston's skyline came into a non-blurred view. Massive shimmering skyscrapers filled the window, many over a hundred stories tall. An intricate network of sky bridges connected the buildings at random intervals, creating an enormous metallic web. A constant stream of commuter shuttles passed in between the structures, servicing the towering pillars of commerce. The faces of countless residents came into focus as the train slowed to a stop. Elegant suits and cutting edge fashion mingled upon a maze of seamless walkways. Hover carts and robotic assistants followed their owners in and out of boutiques. Automated machines with spidery appendages scrubbed external surfaces and pruned beds of foliage. With his eyes fixated on the churning cityscape, Max failed to notice that most of the train passengers had exited.

"The next stop will be the Atlanta Subport with an ETA of 40 minutes," the AI said.

"Shit!" Max jumped to his feet and slipped through the sliding doors just before they closed. "Whew, that was a close one. Got to pay better attention."

"Meow," Ross said in agreement.

The train departed without a sound, leaving them alone on the elevated platform. Max adjusted his backpack and stepped out from underneath the station awning. The warm summer sunshine tickled his face and shoulders, prompting a sigh of satisfaction, then a pucker of confusion.

"Wait, shouldn't it be blistering hot, wretchedly humid, and all-around miserable this time of year? And where's the smell? Last time I was in Houston, it smelled like the sweaty crotch of a sumo wrestler."

"Meow," Ross said, explaining that the combination of clean, renewable energy and atmospheric conditioning kept most of the planet at a balmy 70 degrees.

Max walked to the end of the platform, tromped down the exit stairs, and emerged into a perpetual promenade. Glancing in both directions, he examined the seamless plane. One end disappeared into the city center while the other delved into a suburban jungle. A multitude of jubilant citizens hiked upon its surface, flowing between a vast network of soaring buildings. Planting strips lined the walkways, giving life to colorful bouquets of flowers and a variety of fruit trees. A random passerby plucked a fresh orange on their way to a mystery destination. Following their lead, Max plucked a large red apple from a nearby tree and sank his teeth into one of the most delicious pieces of fruit he had ever tasted. Pausing to savor the realization, he closed his eyes to chew.

As he crunched on the sweet flesh, a dull rumble snaked across the polished concrete. Startled, he spun around before lifting his gaze to the sky. An ascending spaceship broke from the Houston skyline and pierced the clouds. A fluffy exhaust trail poured from the bright yellow glow of two massive engines. The awesome reality of the situation sent chills down his spine. As the liftoff rumble faded, his gaze returned to the city. He traced a wall of glass down to the glowing red logo of the Houston Spaceport entrance about 50 meters away. A toothy smile stretched across his face as a flock of butterflies munched on the apple bits in his stomach.

"Are you ready for this, buddy?" Max said.

"Meow," Ross said, noting his indifference.

Max tossed the apple core into a nearby compost bin and proceeded towards the large glass doors in the distance. Arriving at the entrance, he yanked one of the doors open and stepped into an empty lobby. The hum of a vibrant city faded into the background as the door closed behind him, leaving him alone in a sea of white. The excitement faded from his face as he surveyed the large domed room. Greek-like pillars lined the back wall, serving to highlight the plain, featureless check-in desk resting in front of them. A bright red pillar stood behind the desk. After a lengthy squint, Max confirmed it as human.

"Greetings, traveler," the pillar said with a charming Southern accent. "Welcome to the Houston Spaceport."

"Um, hello," Max said, taking slow steps forward.

As he approached the lonesome desk, the features of a middle-aged woman appeared. Aside from her face, hands, and curly brown hair, every inch of her body hid beneath a fierce red uniform. Max stared at the absurd chef-like hat that clung to her head. A logo pin completed the ensemble.

"My name is Annabelle. How may I help you today?"

"I would like to purchase a one-way ticket to Centauri Station."

"Yes sir, I can help you with that." Lightning-fast fingers pecked at a keyboard hidden behind the desk, her puckered smile never breaking its cemented form. "Alrighty then, the next shuttle will be departing in approximately one hour. You will have a brief layover at Mars Spaceport B before departing for Centauri Station. Will that do?"

"Perfect. And how long is that trip?"

"You should arrive at the Mars port in about two hours, then—"

"Wait ... *two* hours? How is that even possible?"

"Well, sir, per regulation, our shuttles can only legally travel at one-tenth light speed, so it takes a little while."

"A *little* while? They can go even *faster*?"

"Not legally, no. Once you arrive at the Mars port, you will transfer to a cruiser that will also taxi at one-tenth light speed until it passes Neptune's orbit. Only at that point can the craft jump to hyperspace. Standard policy."

Max stood motionless, once again with mouth agape.

"Sir, are you okay?"

"Yes, sorry." Max cleared his throat. "Just a little tired I guess."

"And I see you will be traveling with an adorable pet companion today?"

"Meow," Ross said, confirming the question.

"Yes, and I understand there's a fee?"

"Yes sir, a modest fee that covers the cybernetic body along with consciousness transfer and the first month of cryogenic storage. If you wish to continue past one month of storage, then we will need a credit account on file."

Max added a pair of scrunched eyebrows to his baffled stare and dangling jaw. As his brain struggled to process the last few sentences, it decided to send a placeholder to his mouth. "Uh ... what?"

"Oh, I do apologize. The monthly maintenance account is a new policy."

"No, um, I mean, I can't just bring him with me as is?"

"No sir. Pet travel falls under cluster regulation prohibiting non-humanoid creatures from venturing into space. This prevents the possible spread of communicable diseases. Pets are required to utilize artificial bodies while traveling off-planet."

Max stared at Annabelle as if she had just described the nuances of quantum physics.

"Meow," Ross said, apologizing for his doltish owner.

"Wow, um ... I just, okay." Max took a deep breath and tried to expel the awkward tension. "So, um, how does that work?"

Annabelle huffed and blinked her eyes a few times too many. "Sir, I do not have time to explain the intricacies of cybernetic transfer."

Max glanced around the still empty room. "But I'm the only one here."

Annabelle, her pursed smile now sans smile, let out a disgruntled sigh. She leaned to the side and peered over Max's shoulder in hopes of uncovering a mounting line, but found no such luck. She sneered at Max, then lowered her gaze to the monitor. A hologram video feed appeared above the desk after some heavy finger pecking. With an over-exaggerated arm drop, she pressed a final key.

A pleasant jingle sounded as a plain-suited man blinked onto the screen. "Greetings, traveler. Welcome to CounterPet Incorporated, the leading experts in pet-based cryogenics." A comical rendition of a dog and cat appeared on the screen, smiling and playing as the narrator continued his spiel. "Here at CounterPet, we take excellent care of your furry friends while you are away. Our advanced cryogenic facility protects and stores your pet's physical body while its consciousness lives on inside a cybernetic replica." Colorful pop-up diagrams appeared in manners that would please a small child. "Our patented 3D printing technology can assemble your replica in a few short minutes, all while you wait. And when you return from your trip, we simply transfer the consciousness back to the physical body.

You can even keep the cybernetic shell as a nifty souvenir. Feel free to ask your travel agent for more details. CounterPet, keeping your companions close."

The hologram blinked away before the outro melody completed, revealing the irritated face of Annabelle. "Will that be all, sir?"

"Meow," Ross said, eager to get the show on the road.

Max, his face now wearing a confounded expression, could not help but blurt out the one burning question on his mind. "Can humans do that?"

Annabelle tightened her face. "Do what?"

He pointed at the empty space above the desk as if the video was still streaming. "The cyborg thing."

"No, of course not. It's against cluster policy."

"Why?"

"Is it not obvious?"

"Apparently not," Max said, lowering his eyelids to half-mast.

"Let's just put it like this. Think of the stupidest person you know. For many, I'm sure that's you. Now make them Iron Man."

"Oh." Max glanced away in defeat.

"So, once again, will that be all?" Annabelle's widened eyes hurled daggers at Max, conveying a complete lack of patience.

Max lifted the carrier and peeked inside at Ross, who had taken the opportunity to catch a nap. A grin lifted from Max's chin as his buddy rolled onto his back and stretched his legs into the side of the carrier. "Yes, let's do this."

"Very good, sir. Now, if you would please look at me for a moment."

Max responded with a blank stare.

Annabelle sighed and lifted an iris scanner. After a ping of acceptance, her annoyed gaze fell to the monitor. Furious hands input all the necessary info. "I assume you would like English as a default?"

"For what?"

Annabelle rolled her eyes. "For your cat."

"Wait, what? He'll be able to *speak*?"

She glanced away for a moment, as if to relay disgust to a nonexistent colleague. "Of course. All CounterPets come with language capabilities. You get one free default with the option to add more for extra fees."

"English will be fine."

Annabelle returned her gaze to the monitor and pecked her keyboard with a mounting agitation. "Would you like an accent for a small fee?"

Max burst into laughter, causing Annabelle to flinch. "Now you're just messing with me."

She glared at Max with the icy stare of a serial killer.

His chuckle shrunk into the lowered chin of a chastised child. After a moment of contemplation, a half-smile crept up his cheek. "Um, British please."

Without a word, she input the rest of the required info. "Oh, for pity's sake." Annabelle huffed with peak irritation. "I regret to inform you that the Mars pattern is full for the next several hours. We can, however, reroute you through Europa with a 10-hour layover. You will not lose too much time, if you wish to depart within the hour."

"Europa? As in Jupiter's Europa?" A toothy smile filled his face, but slammed shut when confronted by the angered death stare of Annabelle. "Yes, that will be fine."

She entered the final confirmation. "Okay sir, you have been checked in for your trip to Centauri Station. Now, if you would be so kind as to take your pet to the waiting area behind this wall, a CounterPet representative will meet you with further instructions. On behalf of everyone here at the Houston Spaceport, I hope you have a safe and wonderful trip." Annabelle offered a smirk of conclusion that in no way matched her cold stare.

"So how do I—" Max said, but Annabelle's widening eyes cut him off. "Nevermind. Thank you." Max lowered his gaze to the ground and walked around the corner.

"Meow," Ross said, thanking her for the assistance.

* * *

"*That* is Jai Ferenhal?" Perra said, lowering her voice to a harsh whisper.

"In the flesh," Zoey said.

"He's coming this way."

"Listen." Zoey's voice dropped into a commanding tone, snapping Perra to attention. "Whatever happens, let me do the talking. Do not engage with him in any way. If things get stirred, I want you to get back to the ship and make for Marcoza. I'll catch up with you there. Understand?"

"Y—yes." Perra bowed her head and took a deep breath.

"Well if it isn't Zoey Bryx and her little whore," Jai said in a gruff voice as he sauntered up to the booth. He swirled the drink in his hand, clinking ice cubes against the stumpy glass.

"Jai," Zoey said with a flat tone. She lifted a sharpened gaze to the grinning brute.

Perra sat still with her head lowered. Jai looked her up and down, huffed in disregard, then parked next to her in the booth. His muscular frame pushed her into the window, prompting a faint whimper. Zoey never broke eye contact.

"Thanks for the drink," Jai said to Zoey, taking a sip of his expensive cocktail. "Although, I would have appreciated something else."

"You have no claim to that particular something."

"Says you. Lord Essien says differently."

Zoey's lower lip dropped open for a split second.

Jai noticed and smirked. "So, The Omen *can* flinch."

"You're working for *Essien*?"

"What can I say, she made me a lucrative offer."

Zoey leaned back in the booth, crossed her arms, and tightened her face in disgust. "You know, I can understand someone like you betraying the PCDS. I can even understand, to a point, you joining the Veiled Traders. But to work for Essien? What in the 'verse went wrong for you to end up under that psycho's thumb?"

"Does it matter? Business is business."

"No." Zoey shook her head. "You have taken this to an entirely new level."

"Regardless, my sweet, Essien wants a piece now." Jai took another sip and hardened his glare. "So, you need to deliver, or face the consequences."

Perra lifted a worried gaze to Zoey, who urged her to remain calm with a subtle gesture.

"That deal is done," Zoey said. "You know that."

"Then undo it." Jai tossed back the remainder of his drink and clanked the empty glass upon the table. "Don't care how."

"And if I can't?"

"Then you can tell Essien herself. She will arrive in half a poch."

Zoey's eyes widened. "Essien is coming *here*?"

"You have until then to make arrangements." Jai caressed Perra's thigh as he lifted from the booth, causing her to recoil. He straightened his suit jacket and sneered at Zoey. "Also, if you're thinking of doing something stupid, like leave, know that we have three assault ships in orbit with a lock on that pitiful excuse for a freighter." Jai winked at Perra, then turned and exited the bar.

CHAPTER 7

Max knocked his knees together from the confines of an uncomfortable plastic chair. The molded white butt-cup and its wobbling metal legs seemed to struggle with his below-average weight. Every movement creaked and scraped upon the cold linoleum floor. An invisible cloud of pungent chemicals assaulted his nose from every direction, creating the needless tension of a dentist's office. His backpack bounced upon his thighs as his mind concocted a reasonable quiz. Before taking Ross into the rear facility, the CounterPet representative instructed Max to devise three personal questions that only he and Ross could answer, ensuring a successful transmission of consciousness.

"They're almost done," said a young woman minding the reception desk. "Just another minute or two."

Max nodded and allowed his eyes to wander around the simplistic lobby. A row of six matching chairs sat in front of a large clouded glass pane, separating the facility from the spaceport terminal. The low ceiling, with its diffused light and industrial paneling, served to exacerbate any feelings of claustrophobia. A basic and boring reception desk sat off-center along the rear wall, infecting the space with a callous indifference to interior design. A small picture frame atop the desk housed the company logo. The receptionist herself served as the only pop of color, her silky pink blouse and purple jacket reflecting off the clouded glass. Aside from a wall-mounted brochure rack, the entire room gave off an unsettling vibe of incompleteness.

A pair of faint voices echoed from the hallway behind the reception desk. As they neared the lobby, Max could distinguish between the representative and a somewhat familiar British accent.

"Oi, Max!" Ross emerged from the hallway and trotted across the room.

"Holy crap, hey buddy." Max reached down to pet his furry companion, then lifted an astonished gaze to Kenneth, the smiling representative with balding red hair, starched white lab coat, and horn-rimmed glasses. "I can't tell a difference. He feels just like he did before."

"He *is* the cat he was before," Kenneth said. "Think of it as transferring a hard drive from one computer to another. Everything that made the computer useful and unique has been retained. He just has better hardware now."

"Speaking of which," Ross said to Max. "Kenny gave me a whole bunch of useful info about maintenance, which, for the most part, is none at all. I can even generate my own energy through electromagnetic radiation."

"You're solar powered?"

"No, I'm wind-powered. Do you even science?"

Max sighed and turned to Kenneth. "So he doesn't need food or water anymore?"

"Yes and no. He has a synthetic digestive system in place that performs the exact same functions as a natural one. He can still eat, drink, and excrete, as well as derive energy from the activity. However, it is only supplemental, not critical."

"In other words, I can still force you to scoop the litter box," Ross said.

Max sneered in response.

"He also has an internal battery storage that can last for several months when fully charged," Kenneth said. "Plus, the photovoltaic material used for his exterior is resistant to the elements. He can get wet and lie in the sun for as long as he wants without any ill effects."

"Not that I would ever yearn for a swim," Ross said.

They all shared a polite chuckle.

"So, one final order of business and you can be on your way," Kenneth said. "Have you prepared three questions for Ross?"

"Yes."

"Very good. In that case, please proceed."

Ross jumped onto an adjacent chair and took a seat facing Max.

"Okay, question one. What is the name of our neighbor's cat?"

"Gerald. Good lad, that one."

"Good. Next question. Who do you hate most in this world?"

"Your mum," Ross said with a straight face. "Ha, just taking the piss. That would be Megan, your chore of an ex-girlfriend."

"Good." Max rolled his eyes. "Last question. Who gives you those little foam soccer balls for Christmas every year?"

"Your mum." Ross ruffled his brow. "That one I meant."

"Good job, buddy." Max scratched his head and lifted his gaze to Kenneth. "Nailed them all."

"I'm not surprised," Kenneth said with a satisfied smile. "It's exceedingly rare for a transfer to fail. The technology these days is as reliable as it is sophisticated."

Max nodded and turned to Ross. "Well if you're happy, then I'm happy."

"Are you kidding? This is the dog's bollocks. Or the cat's meow, if you prefer. Stupid expression to be honest. What intrinsic value can be placed on the generic vocalization of a cat? We don't even meow at each other, so why is it so important? It's the humans who value the cat's meow, not the cats. Bunch of wankers you are."

Max sighed. "Doesn't get more Ross than that."

"Heather has a release form for you to sign and then you're free to go. Ross, you be good."

"Can't promise anything, Kenny," Ross said with a sly wink.

Kenneth snort-laughed and adjusted his glasses.

Max lifted from the chair and slung his backpack over a shoulder.

"Thank you very much, sir," Max said, giving Kenneth a firm handshake.

"My pleasure, and you two have a safe trip."

Kenneth nodded goodbye and disappeared down the hallway. Max approached the reception desk and signed a digital release form that Heather had prepared. A ping of acceptance concluded the visit. She plucked a business card from the desktop and handed it to Max.

"A transaction receipt and transfer report have been linked to your travel account. Please feel free to contact us at any time should Ross experience any issues."

"I will, thank you." Max turned to leave, but caught himself. "Oh, my carrier."

"We store that for you until you return, unless you need it for another purpose. Now that Ross has sentient speech, he can walk on his own in public. However, you are his legal guardian and must govern him accordingly."

"Well bully for me," Ross said, jumping down from the chair.

"Understood," Max said, then turned to Ross. "Are you ready to roll, buddy?"

"Indeed, my friend. Off to Europa!"

* * *

Zoey and Perra stormed into their suite. "You have to talk to me, Zoey," Perra said as the door closed behind them. "I knew you had a history with Jai, but that sounded way too serious for a courier quarrel." Zoey nabbed her bag from the entrance table and tossed it onto the bed. "What was Jai talking about? Do you know something about the cargo that I don't?" A laser-focused Zoey unzipped the bag and began to assemble bits of composite. "And who is this Lord Essien? She sounds like one serious twat."

With a final click of a completed plasma gun, Zoey spun around to Perra and lifted a stiff hand into the air. "Perra, you have to stop. Yes, this is serious, more than you could ever imagine. I do not have time to explain, but I will later, I promise. Right now, we have one and only one priority: get the hell off this moon before Essien arrives."

"But how?" Perra swung her arms open. "You heard Jai. They have assault ships right above us."

"That's why I need *you*." Zoey handed Perra the plasma gun. Its elliptical body and iridescent guts twisted light like a prism. PCDS couriers favored the deconstructible models for obvious reasons. As high-profile targets, their preparation was paramount.

Perra accepted the weapon with a cautious hand. "How the hell did you get this through security?"

"Military-grade composite, no metal or registry chips, invisible to scanners." Zoey started to assemble a second weapon.

Perra took a deep breath and lowered the weapon to her side. "Okay, so what do you need me to do?"

"Like I said, we need to get off this rock. So, we need an exit strategy. The rules are simple. One, we can't leave the cargo. Two, we can't die." With a final click of the completed second weapon, Zoey returned her attention to Perra and gave her a thumbs-up. "And, go."

Perra smacked her forehead with her non-weaponized hand and slid it down her face, ending with a scornful gaze. After a heavy sigh, she began pacing around the room. Nervous fingers brushed along swanky furnishings, derailing her concentration for brief moments. She strolled past enormous windowpanes that overlooked Europa's icy surface, pausing to trace the stark horizon as it sliced through Jupiter's massive visage. The corner of her mouth pursed with a partial smile as she glanced into a luxurious bathroom decked out with posh Italian tile. Burnished nickel fixtures gleamed in the soft light of intricate wall sconces. She eyed several pieces of fine art adorning the stone-faced interior, inscribed with the looping signatures of renowned artists. Her gaze lifted to the vaulted ceiling, painted with the greens and blues of a massive abstract mural. "Sweet mercy this room is nice."

"Perra, focus," Zoey said with a curt tone.

"Sorry, sorry." Perra groaned and plopped onto the bed. Her

body sank into the soft and luscious memory material. "Ooo, very nice."

"Perra!"

"Bah, sorry."

Zoey started pacing around the room as well, racking her brain for a solution to their perilous predicament. Her wandering eyes also caught the elegant furnishings and upper mural before coming to a stop in front of the giant windows. "Wow."

"I know, right?"

"Ugh." Zoey shook her head and pulled her hair in an effort to refocus. She fished the comdev from her pocket and placed it face-up on the nearest table. After a few taps of input, the device pinged for voice command. "Europa atmo traffic. Color IDs." A small holographic image of the moon appeared over the device, complete with an array of colored dots hovering around it; yellow for satellites, green for civilian ships, blue for service vessels, red for weaponized ships. "There." Zoey pointed at a small cluster of three red dots. "Jai isn't lying." With a quick tap and finger spread, she zoomed into the vicinity, bringing the assault ships into gridded detail. She huffed and lowered her chin. "You have got to be kidding me."

"What?" Perra said, now sprawled out on the bed.

"Those aren't assault ships." Zoey closed her eyes and let out a heavy sigh. "We may have been able to handle assault ships. Those are Black Razor ships."

Perra gasped and yanked herself up. "Rippers?!"

Zoey lifted a tormented gaze to the ceiling and ran both hands through her choppy black hair. "Oh Jai, what have you gotten yourself into?"

* * *

Max sipped on his third cup of coffee as Ross groomed his artificial fur in the seat beside him. The terminal of the Houston Spaceport reminded him of the crude airports he already knew. He surveyed the open air of the multi-level complex before lifting his eyes to the ceiling. Large panes of acrylic glass formed a massive arch far above, illuminating the terminal with warm natural light. The occasional shuttle punched through the cloudline, drawing the attention of waiting passengers. Max lowered his gaze to the second-floor railings that secured numerous shops and diners. A variety of gadget kiosks and coffee bars peppered the first-floor corridor.

Max took another sip of coffee and glanced down each end of the terminal. He leaned back in his seat and marveled at the distinct lack of human traffic. He and Ross found themselves all but alone in a crop of cozy waiting chairs. A handful of bored travelers ducked in and out of shops or stopped for coffee. Max counted a few dozen heads rising above an open field of seating. A quiet calmness seemed to engulf the great hall, like riding an elevator on a much grander scale. Spaceports came with an unspoken rule of civility that no one dared to challenge. Max found it quite refreshing; no crying babies with indifferent mothers, no tactless pricks yelling into cell phones, no entitled tourists barking at service personnel, no beeping carts hauling obese gluttons to their gates. A peculiar new thought popped into his mind. Max crossed his arms and nodded with approval. *Hassle-free travel. What a truly wonderful world.*

"Attention, traveler," said a breathy feminine voice into his ears, jolting him from thought. He spun to address the source, but found nobody there. "We are about to commence boarding for the 3:10 shuttle to Europa. Please proceed to gate 4A."

Max twisted from side to side in confusion. "Ross, did you hear that?"

Ross continued his grooming session unabated.

"Hey, Ross." Max reached over and poked the top of his companion's head.

"What?" Ross jerked his head out of his crotch and glared at Max.

"Did you hear that?"

"Yeah, I heard it. Time to go."

"Then why didn't you answer me?"

"I tune you out when addressing important things."

"Like licking yourself?"

"Precisely. Any more questions?"

"Yeah, who the hell whispered into my ear?"

"I did," the voice said.

Max jerked his arms into a karate stance.

"My name is Helena. I am the Houston Spaceport management system. I use localized audio transmissions to keep you informed no matter where you are inside the terminal."

"Um ... thanks?" Max said, still ready for battle.

"You are most welcome, kind traveler. Now please proceed to gate 4A. Your shuttle will board shortly."

"Yes, ma'am."

Max stood from his seat and eyed the open air like a paranoid schizophrenic. While maintaining eye contact with nothing in particular, he nabbed his backpack from the adjoining seat and slung it over his shoulder. Ross jumped down from his own seat and trotted towards the gate. Max launched into a light jog to keep up with his furry friend, but paused in confusion once they arrived at the gate.

Ross stopped and turned around. "What's wrong now?"

"Where's the ticket person? There's nobody here. There's no security or anything."

"What are you talking about?"

"Who's to stop someone from wandering onto the shuttle?"

"That's impossible. The spaceport AI monitors everyone at all times. It knows who has access to what and governs them accordingly. It can assess all sorts of things, like if you have any diseases that can't leave the planet. It can even determine if you're psychologically fit to fly. To be honest, I'm shocked it hadn't stopped *you* yet."

"Oh." Max thought for a second. "That's a much better system than before."

Ross tilted his head. "What?"

"Nothing. Don't worry about it, Garfield."

"That's racist."

Max chuckled to himself as they joined a handful of other travelers walking down a covered gangway to the steaming side of a space shuttle. Deciding to roll with the punches, Max tried to blend in by mimicking his fellow passengers. For the most part, travelers remained calm and indifferent, as if dropping by the corner store to pick up a carton of milk. Max struggled to contain his mounting excitement. He battled a potent urge to shake his nearest neighbor and howl with glee. Each step brought him closer to a seamless white shuttle resting on its belly. No boosters or launch pad, just a regular plane-like stance that allowed occupants to settle into their seats upright. Nearing the hatch, he studied the retractable landing gear protruding from the hull, giant metal claws that gripped the smooth pavement like a gecko. The vehicle resembled a polished, corporatized version of an old NASA space shuttle with red wing tips and logoed siding. Max's inner child screamed with elation as he neared the end of the gangway.

Stepping through the hatch, Max scanned the shuttle's interior with the bulging eyes of a giddy schoolgirl. The moderate-sized vehicle housed many familiar features of the planes he knew; rows of seats with window ports, overhead bins for portable luggage, a small panel of boxy control buttons, even strips of safety lights running the length of the center aisle. The shuttle also offered notable improvements. The horror cages of claustrophobic torture, also known as airline seats, had been replaced by plush lounging chairs; plush to the point of ridiculousness even by the first-class standards he knew. Seats numbered about 20 in total with two rows on either side of the cabin.

His eight fellow passengers selected their preferred seats, secured bags overhead, and settled into form-fitting leathery cushions. Max opted for a front seat after a few moments of unnecessary contemplation. With his backpack secured overhead, he sank into the doughy cushions and let out a grunt of satisfaction. Limp hands stroked the synthetic fabric like a garish villain with a hairless pet. The seat auto-adjusted its external temperature to a cozy degree, eliciting a moan of contentment. Ross jumped onto his lap and began kneading his thigh.

"I'm in an actual space shuttle," Max said before letting out a snorting chuckle.

"You say that like you've never done this before."

"I haven't."

Ross paused and scrunched his brow. "Should I ask or do I care?"

"You didn't seem to care before."

"You're right, I don't care." He unclenched his face and returned to the kneading.

A hard thump echoed through the cabin as the flight attendant sealed the hatch. She straightened her pressed blue uniform before turning to face the passengers. A quick tap of her jacket collar activated the intercom system.

"Good afternoon, passengers," she said, sending her pleasant voice through the cabin. "My name is Eleanor and I will be your flight attendant for your short trip to Europa. We are almost ready for liftoff, so at this time we request that you secure your seat belts. If you need any assistance, please press the call button overhead."

Max raised his hand.

Eleanor glanced at him, but did not move or respond.

"Press the call button, goober," Ross said.

"But she's literally five feet in front of me." Max gestured with an open palm.

"Protocol, you idiot."

Max sighed and pressed the yellow call button above his head.

"Yes sir, how may I be of assistance?" Eleanor broke out of her statue-like stance to offer a forced smile.

"Do I just hold my cat in my lap?"

"That would be advised, yes."

"And how do I go about that?"

"I would use your hands." Eleanor blinked several times, showing impatience through her cemented expression.

Max huffed. "No, I mean, do you have a strap I should use or something?"

"You can request a pet harness if you would like."

"That won't be necessary," Ross said, still kneading.

"But what if I lose my grip and you bounce around all over the cabin?"

Ross glared up at Max. "This is a shuttle, nimrod. Not the Apollo mission."

"Fine." Max slap-gripped the armrests and returned his gaze to Eleanor. "No harness, I'm good, thank you."

"Very good, sir. Now if you would fasten your seat belt, we can get underway."

Max glanced behind him for sympathy and noticed that all eyes had fixated hateful stares upon him.

"Ah, so I'm the asshole," he said under his breath as he buckled his seat belt.

"Okay, ladies and gentlemen, we have been cleared for departure. Our flight time will be approximately five and a half hours. Once we have exited the atmosphere, I will be serving a variety of refreshments. For now, just sit back, relax, and enjoy liftoff."

With a ping of conclusion, Eleanor took her seat at the front of the vehicle and buried her nose into an ebook. The gangway retracted itself as a muted rumble snaked its way across the cabin. The Houston Spaceport sank away from the windows as hull thrusters lifted the shuttle from its perch. The vessel rotated skyward, pressing Max into the back of his seat and Ross into his stomach. The main engines ignited, sending a gentle jolt down the fuselage. A giant, toothy grin filled Max's face as the craft climbed into the atmosphere.

"Woooo!" Max shot his arms into the air as if riding a rollercoaster. He glanced back at his fellow spacefarers, hoping to share his excitement. Annoyed stares from atop ebooks and hologram feeds returned no such sentiment. A few passengers had already fallen asleep.

"Rein it in, jackass," Ross said from a curled pile in his lap.

Max's elated expression faded from his face, but a giddy smirk remained. He turned his attention to the window, which faded to black after a few seconds. Countless stars appeared and shimmered with a crystal clarity he had never experienced on Earth. His eyes glued themselves to the glass as his jaw lowered at a snail's pace.

"I barely felt a thing," Max said.

Ross responded with a light snore.

Max smiled and placed a gentle hand upon his furry friend. Peering behind the vessel, he watched the Earth, his home, the only surface he had ever known, fade into a pale blue dot.

CHAPTER 8

Zoey tapped her chin with a nervous finger as she paced around the luxurious suite. Perra filled an armchair in the corner, leaning forward with elbows propped on her knees. She stared at the floor through barren eyes, contemplating options. Restless hands passed the plasma gun back and forth, its smooth composite shell reflecting Jupiter's pastel colors from the giant windowpanes.

"This could work," Zoey said.

Perra leaned back in the chair, dropped the plasma gun on a side table, and covered her face with both hands. "I'm sorry, my love, but I don't share your confidence."

"No, this has promise. Let's go over it again."

Perra sighed, slapped her hands onto the armrests, and motioned to Zoey with a limp wrist. "Fine, proceed."

"Okay, so, we both leave here dressed in formals as to not raise any unwanted suspicion. We know that Jai and his posse will be watching our every move, so we don't bother hiding from them. He needs to remain anonymous in a place like this. Veiled Traders on Europa would not bode well for his reputation, so we can use that to our advantage. If we can get to the lobby entrance without incident, that should give us the time we need."

Perra lifted a worried gaze to Zoey. "We are going to be so exposed."

"I know." Zoey lowered her chin and nodded. "Doesn't matter though, all we need is a solid head start."

"Fair enough." Perra crossed her arms and stared at the floor.

"If I know Jai as well as I think I do, he will have a few lackeys stationed somewhere near the entrance, probably dressed as business types. Hopefully, they will stick out enough for us to pinpoint. We need to lock eyes with any that lock on us. Know who they are. The last thing we need is the death of an innocent."

Perra gave a slow nod as Zoey resumed her pacing.

"From here, we walk straight to the front entrance, no dallying. When they confront us, the show begins. As soon as I fire the first shot, the whole place is going to erupt in chaos. You run as fast as you can to the ship and spin up the jump drive. I'll keep those assholes busy until you're ready. And once I'm inside with the airlock sealed, we thrust the ship's nose to a patch of black and jump. That should give us enough time to avoid the Rippers."

Perra took a deep breath and shook her head. "This is so risky."

Zoey stopped pacing and glared at Perra. "But you said this was perfectly feasible. We don't need the main engines to jump into hyperspace."

"Feasible, yes, but incredibly dangerous." Perra stood from her seat. "You need the main engines for stabilization, otherwise you can come out the other end in an uncontrolled spin. And that's without destination coordinates. Who's to say we don't end up in an asteroid field with nothing but thrusters? I understand that we need to sacrifice prep for time, but this is a jump into the black with no beacon of any kind. Again, feasible, but completely insane." Perra slogged over to the windows and placed both hands on her hips. She expelled a heavy sigh while overlooking the icy landscape. "Furthermore, our ship is secured to the station dock. You know the port authority will lock down detachments if we start shooting up the place, which kind of nulls the escape plan."

Zoey smirked. "But we don't need to detach."

Perra turned to Zoey and lifted an eyebrow. "What, do you plan on taking the entire Europa Center with us?"

"No, just the dock seal. We have atmo locks and flash gel on the ship, do we not?"

Perra returned the smirk. "Very clever, you sultry minx."

* * *

Max's heart seemed hell-bent to escape his chest as he gazed upon the enormous gas giant through the window port. Jupiter's massive vista bathed his face in creamy pastels, its swirling ribbons twisting and turning over each other in a slow yet violent dance. The great red eye churned in the southern hemisphere, serving to highlight the raw power of the universe and humanity's lack of meaningful influence.

A bead of saliva broke free of Max's dangling lip and landed on Ross's ear.

"Did you just—eeew," Ross said. He shook his head and flung his own saliva in retaliation.

"Ugh, thanks for that." Max wiped his cheek.

"Attention, passengers," Eleanor said, now standing upfront with a plastic expression. "We have begun our descent to Europa and will dock in about 20 Earth minutes. At this time, please return to your seats and stow any loose items for arrival." Max glanced at the rear of the shuttle where nobody had moved since liftoff. "Once we have established a successful seal, the captain will turn off the seat belt sign and you will be free to depart the vessel. For any passengers with connections, you may consult our comdev portal or the numerous atmo traffic panels inside the Europa Center. As always, we thank you for flying with Sigma Starliners and wish you the very best on your continued journey." She tapped the intercom link on her collar, dropped the act, and returned to her seat to resume a game on her comdev.

The cabin lights illuminated, causing passengers to stir in their seats and expel grumbling yawns. Blips of portable devices powering down bounced around the cabin.

"I guess some things never change," Max said to himself.

Returning his gaze to the window, he watched the snowy dome of Europa rise from beneath the shuttle. He pressed his nose to the glass and glanced down at a sea of jagged glaciers and cobalt crevasses. Specks of brown rock littered the landscape, serving as a solitary contrast to the bright surface. In the distance, the sharp edges of an aqua green structure, the Europa Center Station, rested atop a massive white pillar. An intricate spiderweb of clear docking tunnels spilled from the entrance, resembling a crystalline snowflake hovering above the moon's surface. An exotic collection of spaceships with bold colors and sleek hulls docked and disconnected from the snowflake; the kind of ships that screamed opulence, even to someone with no knowledge of spaceships. Some departed for orbit while others disappeared below the station as valets escorted them to long-term parking.

"We there yet?" Ross said, lifting himself into an arched stretch.

"Almost. I can see the station in the distance."

"Okay, wake me up when we dock." Ross dropped into a pile upon Max's lap.

"Wait a minute." Max lowered a skeptical gaze to Ross. "Do you even need to sleep as a CounterPet?"

"Of course not. I just didn't feel like listening to your wack talk for five hours."

"You're such a loving companion." Max returned his gaze to the viewport.

"I'm a cat, not your therapist."

A few minutes later, a slight nudge secured the shuttle onto one of several docking ports along a busy arm of the snowflake. The dull hum of the engines faded away as the seat belt sign overhead pinged off. A rustle of passengers filled the cabin as they gathered their belongings to depart the vessel. Ross jumped to the floor as Max arose from his seat. He retrieved his backpack from an overhead bin and slung it over his shoulder. Eleanor unlocked the hatch and swung it open, resulting in a puff of decompression. The brilliant reflection of

Europa's frigid landscape poured into the shuttle, causing passengers to squint as they exited. Max hung back, opting to exit last as a scant courtesy to the other travelers.

"Have a pleasant stay," Eleanor said to the first traveler. "Thank you for flying with us," she said to the next, and so on and so forth. To Max, she offered a cold smile and nothing more.

He stepped outside onto the clear tunnel floor, eliciting a gasp of awe. The rugged Europan surface spread out like a frozen ocean beneath his feet. Max stood motionless in the crowded corridor with his eyes fixated on the floor, like a texting prick oblivious to their surroundings, but convinced of their unique status as the center of the universe. An array of colorful humanoids, both by attire and complexion, passed Max on their ways to and from the Europa Center Station. Some glanced at him with expressions of concern, wondering if someone had lost a pet. The puffs of airlocks opening and closing broke the dull muffles of conversation. Green hologram signs floated overhead, indicating gate numbers and various terminal directions. Ross trotted down the gangway as Max ogled the breathtaking scenery like a dumbstruck drunkard.

"Oi," Ross said with an impatient tone. "You coming or not?"

"Sorry, sorry," Max said as he leapt forward into a light jog. They strolled down the corridor alongside a bizarre assortment of fellow travelers. Max stared at each one with the bulging eyes of a child in a strip club. "Dude, there are *aliens* everywhere."

"Why are you whispering? Do you not think they know?"

"I don't want to offend anyone."

"Your casual racism never ceases to amaze me."

"My cas—I'm not a racist."

"Yet you whisper among them without realizing you *are* one."

"I just—" Max sighed. "Good point. Touché."

Max's eyes began to wander as the weight of his new reality settled upon his shoulders. His lungs fluttered with excitement; his ears drank the hum of commerce; his nose swam in a sea of compelling new aromas; his mind, despite the overwhelming onslaught of new and exciting stimulus, found itself at ease for the first time in years.

The crowd thickened as they poured into the central corridor, a widened channel serving as the main terminal throughput. High-end kiosks sat along the walls, offering a variety of exclusive products. Blue-skinned humanoids in gray uniforms tended to each station, greeting each passerby with warm smiles and kind words. Iris scanners pinged with purchase confirmations. The occasional gasp of admiration spilled from jewelry counters. The hiss of espresso machines complemented puffs of rising steam. With his gaze locked onto the blackness of space above, Max's shoulder collided with another.

"Watch it, skinbag," a suited humanoid said through a yellow, scaled expression.

"Sorry," Max said, jumping aside to avoid the growing flow of foot traffic. He ducked into an open section between kiosks, pausing to rest.

"What is wrong with you today?" Ross said, shooting a sour glance up to Max.

Max turned to face the wall and studied the sliver of Europa's horizon. He placed an open hand upon the clear composite, allowing a hint of coolness to penetrate his skin. His head lifted to digest the monstrous dome of Jupiter towering over the landscape. It dwarfed the moon in every possible manner, superimposed atop a sheet of twinkling black. With his eyes beginning to water, Max grinned with a healthy dose of serenity. "Ross, my good buddy, this is, by far and away, the best day of my life."

A series of deafening booms erupted from the Europa Center entrance about 50 meters away, sending shockwaves of static down the central corridor. The screams of terrified travelers filled the tunnels. Countless bodies crumpled to the floor while others scattered for shuttles and exits. More static bursts followed, hurling beams of purple light down the composite walls. Max fell to the ground and covered his head. The odors of welding fumes and singed meat infected the sterile air.

"Shit, shit, shit," Ross said as his poofed body scampered down an adjacent tunnel.

"Ross!" Max jumped to his feet to give chase.

Another blast, closer this time, followed by a rumble underfoot and a fresh batch of screams. The entire gangway shook and creaked, causing Max to stumble and catch himself. He glanced back at the central corridor, uncovering little more than white smoke and the shadows of fleeing bodies. A shot of adrenaline kept him sprinting towards the orange ball of frightened fur in the distance. Ross came to a stop at the last airlock, pinning his body against the external hull of a rather unassuming freighter vessel. Max arrived moments later and dropped to his knees to scoop up his fearful friend, but flailing claws and screeching meows conveyed a clear intention of staying put. Another series of booms and screams echoed through the tunnels. Realizing that curiosity would indeed kill the cat, Ross cocked his ears back and started clawing at the vessel door. The airlock slid open and Ross darted inside the ship.

"Goddamnit, Ross!"

Max stood outside the airlock, panting with hesitation. He turned back to the unfolding scene, only to stare down the barrel of Perra's plasma gun. He shot his hands into the air, keeping them tight around his head as if to acknowledge a tiny field goal. His saucer-like eyes seemed more taken aback by her creamy orange complexion than by the pulsing weapon pointed at his face. A glitzy necklace lifted and lowered atop her heaving chest, complementing the swing of sparkling earrings. A swanky blue evening gown hung from her shoulders, its shimmering fabric hugging her hips in perfect symmetry. Perra's piercing eyes softened at the realization of what stood before her.

"My stars ... you're an Earthling," she said as a half-smile crept up her cheek.

"And you most certainly are not," Max said through a shocked expression.

Another series of static booms rumbled down the tunnel, snapping Perra back into duty. She shoved Max aside, slamming his shoulder into the airlock. "Get your damn animal off my ship," she said before darting around the corner and into the cockpit. Racing hands powered up the control panel, filling the cockpit with a warm yellow glow. She keyed a short sequence of commands and thumped a palm down on a large green icon, prompting hull thrusters to ignite underfoot. An empty red bar denoting jump drive readiness began to turn itself green. Perra gnawed on the side of her cheek as she reached overhead to flick a critical string of switches. The sheen of her evening gown reflected pulsing icons around the cockpit.

Max gulped and took a wary step inside the rumbling vessel. He glanced down a narrow passageway leading to the cockpit where Perra's shadowy arms danced across a chirping control panel. Turning to the other side, he found himself standing inside a large cargo bay. LED strips along the ceiling bathed the charcoal gray interior in hygienic light. Roped netting dangled from ceiling hooks, flanking numerous storage compartments that resembled gym lockers. Stacks of logoless crates adorned the metal floor, secured by thick straps and steel latches. The piles provided numerous hiding places for tiny stowaways.

"Ross! Where are you?! Come out here at once!"

"No!" Ross said from somewhere inside, his voice muffled by barriers.

"I mean it! We have to get out of here!"

"What do you think I'm doing?!"

"Get out here! Now! I'm not going to—"

With a violent clunk, Max found himself pinned against the wall of the cargo bay, staring down the barrel of Zoey's plasma gun. A ritzy black dress swung from her waist, exposing her orange thighs as she pressed a forearm into Max's chest.

"Who the hell are you?!" Zoey said.

"Uh ... Max." His eyes shifted from side to side. "The Earthling."

"He's looking for his pet," Perra said from the cockpit.

"That would be me," Ross said from somewhere inside.

Zoey's eyes danced between Perra, Max, and the mystery voice. She huffed and released her hold, sending Max to the metal floor with a sharp clank. Dropping to a knee, she opened one of several floor compartments and fished inside, nabbing a puck-like disc and a tarnished device that resembled a painting gun. Footsteps echoed in the tunnel as Zoey rushed back to the airlock. Blasts of static thundered through the vessel as she fired her plasma gun at Jai's cronies. Max cowered on the ground beside her and covered his ears, flinching with every shot. The impacts of returned fire boomed inside, shaking the ship and creaking everything metal. Jai and his lackeys ducked out of sight for cover, allowing Zoey to arm the disc and hurl it down the corridor. The disc slid across the smooth composite floor and exploded into a white cloud of atmo-tight foam sealant. The cloud hardened in an instant, sealing the corridor off from the rest of the complex. With Jai and his goons behind a wall of blast-proof foam, Zoey darted into the corridor with the flash gel applicator in hand. She adjusted the ignition timer to a short fuse and squeezed the trigger while swinging her arm in a large circle, coating the interior of the tunnel with a continuous string of red flash gel. The gel smoked and crackled as it began to eat through the tunnel walls. Zoey ran back into the vessel, sealed the airlock, scowled at Max, and joined Perra in the cockpit.

"Are we ready yet?" Zoey said, strapping herself into the pilot's chair.

"Almost there," Perra said, tapping a mess of keys with furious hands.

Targeting sirens howled in the cockpit, flashing red as inbound Rippers launched paralyzer missiles.

"Wait!" Max said from the cargo bay. "I'm still in here!"

"Ignore him!" Ross said, now muffled from a different location.

The jump drive indicator pinged with a full green bar.

"That's it, we're good to go," Perra said.

The cockpit flared as the flash gel ignited in the tunnel, allowing the ship to float free on its thrusters with a sliver of the dock attached.

"No, no, no, no," Max said as he wobbled his way towards the cockpit.

"Incoming," Perra said, pointing to the missile trails speeding towards them.

"Better hold on to something, Earthman," Zoey said and pulled back on the throttle.

The ship lifted its nose to the blackness of space, throwing Max to the back of the cargo bay. He landed with a thud, knocking himself unconscious. Zoey tapped a short sequence of keys into the control panel and slammed a fist upon a large green icon. The tiny freighter vanished into a purple sliver of hyperspace as a barrage of missiles slammed into the moon's surface.

CHAPTER 9

Max awoke to complete darkness under the cool sheets of his bed. The deadweight on his chest stirred as he did before emitting a muted purr. Max placed a gentle hand upon his furry friend and stroked his back. Heavy eyelids slid open, allowing drained eyes to stare at nothing as his mind replayed the events of the previous day. A satisfied grin stretched across his face, for a childhood dream had come true. He basked in the renewed outlook of a cherished new memory. With a hefty sigh, he greeted another uneventful morning.

"Yup, that was a good day," Max said under his breath.

"If you say so," Ross said.

Max's eyes widened, not that anyone could tell. "What the—" A shot of adrenaline bent his torso upwards, tossing Ross to the foot of the bed. Gasps poured from his lungs as eyes twisted around whatever room he occupied.

"Oi, calm down," Ross said with a hint of irritation. "Denchi."

Strips of LED lights along the ceiling responded to the command, revealing a charcoal gray room. Max's frightened eyes darted around the near featureless enclosure. The twin-sized bed he occupied, or a close enough approximation, sat along one wall. An equal amount of open space occupied the other, creating a king-sized cell with a similar height. Thin slivers outlined hidden access panels in the walls. Only the bed, lights, and doorframe broke the smooth planes.

"That's Korish for light," Ross said, donning a gratified grin. "They can install some English commands if we like. I don't know about you, but I'm kind of enjoying the Korish." Ross lifted his gaze to the ceiling. "Fikarek."

The ceiling and rear wall disappeared, exposing the external vista of a massive spiral galaxy, its brilliant arms of blue and purple surrounding a giant ball of white light in the center. The collective brilliance of a trillion stars filled the tiny room. Max yelped, leapt out of the bed, and pressed his back against the door.

"You're perfectly fine, mate," Ross said with a hearty chuckle. "Calm the bloody hell down. The wall and ceiling are still there, just reflecting the external view. Neat, huh?"

"Hoboy," Max said through hurried breaths. He lowered his head and closed his eyes to regain control of his breathing.

Ross cocked his ears back. "Okay, too much stimulus. Deyanea." The wall and ceiling returned to their smooth gray nothingness.

Max bent forward and rested his hands upon his knees. As his breathing returned to a somewhat normal pace, he recognized that a strange fabric hugged his waist, resembling a loose pair of boxers. He pinched and twisted the fabric with his fingers, unable to identify the silky synthetic blend. "Um, where are my clothes?"

"Ponreyka," Ross said, prompting a drawer to shoot out of the wall beside Max.

A violent flinch crumpled his body. "Dammit! Stop that!"

"Sorry," Ross said with a snort of amusement.

Max placed a hand on his thumping chest and lowered his gaze to the drawer. His clothes from the previous day lay cleaned, pressed, and folded inside the backlit compartment alongside his backpack. After a few calming breaths, he lowered a nervous hand into the drawer, as if expecting the garments to attack. He retrieved the items piece by piece and reassembled them upon his body. The synthetic fabrics still seemed foreign to his skin, yet they clung to his body with the comfort of a fleece blanket. The deep brown tones of his trousers infected the sterile gray room with a dirty vibe. His navy blue top served as the only pop of color aside from Ross, even beneath a gray overshirt. The drawer closed itself after he nabbed his boots, as if privy to its lack of further relevance. Max took a wearied seat on the bed and slipped his feet into the sim-leather. His hunched posture amplified the stinging pain in his lower back. He pressed on the base of his spine with a soft palm and grimaced in response.

"How's your back?" Ross said.

"Not well, apparently."

"You did take one hell of a tumble. I'm surprised you didn't break something."

Max indulged in a few core twists and back stretches. After a long sigh of contemplation, he stared at his reflection in the opposite wall. "How am I still here?"

"Because those crafty scraps of hotness got us the hell off Europa."

"No," Max said, ruffling his brow. "I mean, how am I still in space?"

Ross tilted his head. "See previous comment."

* * *

Shifting between parallel universes involved a smattering of quirky little rules. Max, as an unwitting shifter with a unique predicament, never benefited from knowing these rules. The answer to his question lay within the confines of domain, in the sense that shifting only affected the domain of the shifter.

Max had departed planet Earth, the only domain he had ever occupied. In leaving the planet, as well as the solar system, his entire domain had transferred to a tiny freighter vessel floating in the vacuum of space. Therefore, whenever he fell asleep, he awoke to changes unique to that environment and its inhabitants. In this case, a human, a cyborg cat, and a pair of orange lesbians.

In a much-needed stroke of luck, the new universe had offered a mental reprieve in the form of an unseen tweak. Perra, a proud southpaw, had gained a useful amount of ambidexterity, providing her with the unique ability to apply duct tape in any direction.

* * *

Jai Ferenhal stood as a meaty green statue just inside the Europa Center entrance. With a practiced hand, he plucked a handkerchief from his jacket pocket and blotted beads of sweat from his brow. A heavy sigh departed his lungs as he tucked the handkerchief back into his pocket. He glanced down at his gray slacks and crimson boots, double-checking their post-battle presentability. Sweaty palms snaked over one another before coming to a folded rest upon his belt buckle.

An eerie silence filled the evacuated port. Small chunks of rubble rested on the lobby floor, the remnants of plasma gun impacts in the adjacent walls. Thin clouds of dust floated around the once sterile air, unable to escape through the damaged filtration system. Jai stared down the central corridor, studying the abandoned merchant booths in an effort to distract his tortured mind. Lord Essien's battlecruiser had settled into orbit not too long ago. She occupied a soon-to-be docking service shuttle, carrying Jai's unknown fate with her.

Two nervous henchmen dressed in dirty leisure suits stood on either side of Jai, serving to highlight his composed demeanor. One shook with a palpable fright while the other rapped his fingers on a plasma rifle.

"What do you think she'll do, Jai?" the rifle henchman said.

"Shut up," Jai said, maintaining his stare.

"I hope she doesn't do what she did on Torg'vey."

"Shut up."

"Do you think she would? Her temper is the stuff of legends."

"Shut up."

"I mean, if she did, we might as well just shoot ourselves now."

With a flick of the wrist, Jai unholstered his proton pistol and incinerated the pesky henchman with a point-blank shot to the chest. The piercing blast rumbled through the station as an ownerless rifle clanked onto the floor. A small cloud of gray ash enveloped the scene and fell like snow. Jai let out a muffled cough, cleared his throat, and dusted off his suit jacket. After a deep breath, he resumed his cold stare down the corridor. The other minion stopped shaking, opting for less visible forms of paralyzing fear like chattering teeth and an all-consuming desire to be anywhere else.

The gentle thump of a docking shuttle shifted Jai's gaze to a nearby airlock. As the ship settled into position, its ghoulish black hull draped shadows over the clear tunnel. The airlock slid open with a puff of pressurized air. Two members of Lord Essien's Black Guard stepped into the main tunnel, revealing the sharp bones, sunken cheeks, and deep purple skin of Varokin males. Their dark complexions melded into jet-black suits, creating ominous silhouettes in the bright corridor. Silver irises peered over the tops of plasma rifles as they secured the adjacent tunnels. Without a word, one of the guards nodded into the open airlock.

An ethereal figure floated into the tunnel. An elegant blue scarf hung from her neck and flowed down her form-fitting black suit. Her business-like appearance seemed to sharpen the teardrop peak of her purple skull. Inky black lips sliced through the milky white tones of her chin and cheeks. A slow turn of her banded neck revealed Jai in the distance, eliciting a smirk of disgust. Her silvery eyes narrowed beneath their ebon sockets. The hollow clack of heels hitting composite echoed inside the tunnel as she stomped towards Jai with a menacing stride, her guards in tow. His hands tightened as a lump formed in his throat. Lord Essien halted her approach in front of Jai's taut face, close enough to sample his breath. She buried visual daggers into his twitching eye sockets, causing him to swallow with a palpable anxiety.

"What up, dawg?" Lord Essien said, exposing her stark white teeth with a farcical expression.

The comical tone caught Jai off guard, resulting in a dumbfounded look of concern.

"What a stupid expression," she said. "These humans, always butchering their dialects for the sake of some insecure uniqueness. I hate their languages. Every one of them feels like I'm chewing on a hunk of taffy that's trying to escape."

Jai shifted his jaw to the side, unsure of how to respond.

"But enough of this." She waved her hand and turned away.

"Lord Essien, I—"

Essien spun her head around and pierced Jai with a scorching gaze that said nothing short of *how dare you speak to me, you incompetent space maggot.*

Receiving the message loud and clear, he shut his trap and gulped.

Essien smirked and softened her tone. "As I understand it, you let a Mulgawat courier and her prissy puss mechanic slip away with one of the most precious artifacts in all of existence ... the very same artifact that I trusted you to acquire, given your reputation and intimate knowledge of said Mulgawats. Am I mistaken?"

Jai's lower jaw trembled.

"Don't answer. It's a tragic tale that I already know. I just wanted to say it out loud so that the gravity of the blunder could land upon your shoulders."

The other henchman stepped forward. "Lord Essien, allow me to exp—" he said before being incinerated by the blast of a Black Guard plasma rifle.

A tight flinch seized Jai's body, evoking a cold grin from an imposing Lord Essien. Jai closed his eyes and grunted as a second round of gray ash tickled his nostrils.

Lord Essien lowered her brow and voice. "That being said, your very existence depends on the answer to this next question." Both members of the Black Guard turned their weapons to Jai. "Do you, Jai Ferenhal, know where those bitches went?"

Jai looked into Essien's shimmering eyes and nodded.

* * *

The door slid open to Max's room, providing him with yet another fright to his already jittered system. Enduring a fresh round of heavy panting, he jerked his hand to his chest as Perra walked into the room. She had traded her elegant evening gown for rows of gunmetal buckles atop a brown leather vest. Dark blue pants hung from her waist, revealing a strip of creamy orange flesh between the duds. Faint oil stains and numerous snap pockets adorned her legs, ending in a pair of black latch boots. A studded wrist brace, a rusty necklace, and a slick ponytail completed an ensemble that screamed steampunk mechanic. Perra leaned against the adjacent wall, giving Max a once-over before turning her attention to Ross.

"How is he feeling?"

"He's doing better," Ross said. "A little freaked, a little sore, but otherwise good."

Max glanced back and forth between his apparent caretakers and threw his hands into the air. "Why not ask me?"

"Because she obviously views me as the superior intellect," Ross said.

Max shot an annoyed glare at Ross, who responded with a smug smirk.

Perra snickered. "Sorry, Max. Ross has been quite helpful while you were unconscious." With a swing of her hip, she lifted from the wall, stepped over to the bed, and took a seat next to Max. "So how's your back? Do you need anything for the pain?"

"It's fine, I guess." Max rubbed the small of his back. "Thanks anyway."

"You're welcome. And allow me to apologize for earlier. We were under a lot of pressure to leave Europa. We did not intend for you to get caught up in this mess."

"Nor was it my intention to get caught up." Max offered a half-smile. "All things considered, I'm just glad we're okay. My aimless adventure continues."

"You mean *our* aimless adventure," Ross said with a spot of bother.

"Oh, shut up." Max shot another glare at Ross. "You're the reason we're here, Garfield."

"That's racist."

"Speaking of *here*, where is here?" Max said to Perra.

"Oh, we are just outside of galaxy VC-832, what you call Andromeda."

Max's eyes widened as he pointed at the blank gray wall. "*That* ... is the Andromeda Galaxy?"

"Yes," Perra said, glancing at the wall in confusion. "We are on our way to the interior rim to deliver an important package."

With his arm and finger still outstretched, and a jaw that seemed to have thrown in the towel for the day, Max stood from the bed and stepped towards the wall. After battling a sudden onslaught of brain itch, he turned to face Perra. "But how is that even possible? We're like two and a half million light-years from Earth."

"Nothing a competent jump drive can't handle," Perra said with a cool confidence. She crossed her legs and cupped her hands around a knee.

"Oh c'mon," Max said, squinting his eyes. "This isn't science fiction. It's not like we just traveled through a wormhole or anything."

Ross rolled his eyes.

Perra smirked. "No, not exactly. I assume this was your first trip through hyperspace?"

"First time I have ever left Earth," Max said with a twinge of embarrassment.

"Wow," Perra said. She lowered her hands to the bed frame and donned an astonished expression. "No wonder you're all disoriented."

"No, that's just his baseline," Ross said.

Max glared at Ross, who responded with another smug smirk.

"So how does that even work?" Max returned to his seat next to Perra and gave her the undivided attention of a child yearning for story time.

"Good question," Perra said, more than happy to chat about her expertise. She took a deep breath and adjusted her posture to that of a professor. "Jump drives work by locking onto a series of coordinates in open space. We input a set of interlocking distances that denote a single point of fixation. From there, the drive crushes a small clump of hydrogen atoms to create the gravitational equivalent of a neutron star." Perra balled her fists and pantomimed the ongoing explanation. "It then focuses that gravitational pull onto the given coordinates and latches onto whatever is there, usually a neutrino particle, sometimes an atom of hydrogen or helium." Her voice elevated with excitement as she delved into the logistics. "It hooks the fabric of space, like a claw on a blanket, and pulls the particle towards the ship at trillions of times the speed of light. In the process, it warps the region of space the particle occupies. When the particle reaches the ship, the space-time fabric rips, creating a brief hole for the ship to slip through. The rip engulfs the ship and slams shut. From there, the warped space-time fabric snaps back like a rubber band, taking the ship with it."

Ross nodded like a proud sensei as Max's jaw continued its muscle strike.

Perra sighed and folded her hands. "Unfortunately, we did not have time to verify proper coordinates. We could only punch in a distance and cross our fingers. And so, we pointed our nose to the black and grabbed whatever hook we could find. A dangerous maneuver, to say the least. There's no telling what we could have collided with, but we came out okay. Zoey is a great pilot. She stabilized us pretty quick."

Max donned a vacant expression as his sputtering brain sifted through a deluge of questions. His mouth indulged in some freestyle stuttering as he sorted out the most pressing queries. Shaking his head, he settled on what seemed the most pertinent. "Trillions of times the speed of light? How is that possible?"

"Why wouldn't it be?" Perra said with an amused tone.

"Because nothing can travel faster than light," Max said with a limp confidence.

"I think we just proved that wrong," Ross said with a note of sarcasm.

"Why bother explaining it to him?" Zoey said from the doorway. Her form-fitting pilot suit, with a dark gray base tone and midnight blue accents, seemed to complement the sleek-grit contrast of the ship. A single black zipper from waist to neck hung open at her chest, giving a casual vibe to her obvious authority. Her black latch boots matched Perra's, but her heavier stride echoed atop the metal floor panels. Zoey rested a shoulder on the doorframe and glared at Max. "He's an Earthling. Ergo, he suffers from an inferior intellect."

"No arguments here," Ross said.

Max glared at Ross, who responded with yet another smug smirk.

"I think it's cute," Perra said with a lighthearted tone. "He's so naive, it's adorable." She pinched his cheek like a proud grandmother.

Max recoiled and batted her hand away, feeling the sting of emasculation.

Ross decided that imminent grooming duties trumped the remaining conversation.

"Perra, a word," Zoey said with a hardened gaze, then disappeared into the cargo bay.

Perra sighed. "Be right back." Rising from the bed, she gave Max a pat on the shoulder. She walked through the door and met eyes with a perturbed Zoey, standing with arms crossed at the rear of the room. Perra bit the inside of her cheek as she sauntered over to Zoey's tapping foot. "Yes, honey?" she said with a hint of derision.

Zoey switched to Korish to conceal the conversation. "Don't make light of this. We are already dealing with enough without having to look after *them*."

"Oh, lighten up. They aren't harming anything. Max is harmless and Ross is hilarious. To be honest, it's somewhat refreshing having new friends on board."

Zoey narrowed her eyes and took a step towards Perra. "They're not our *friends*, Perra. They're stowaways. Deadweight. Tagalongs that we will dump at the next port. Tagalongs, by the way, that *you* let on board."

Perra extended her chin and scrunched her brow. "Are you saying this is *my* fault, miss get-off-this-rock-at-all-costs? If I recall, it was you and that damn cargo that got us in this mess to begin with."

"Hey, don't you dare put this on me. You know damn well that this job comes with a certain level of risk."

"Risk? *Risk?*" Perra took a step forward, bringing them face-to-face. "I can handle risk. That clusterfuck of insanity we just escaped from was beyond risk." She pointed a firm finger to the airlock. "We still have part of the Europa Center dock attached to our ship. What on Tim's Blue Terra are we carrying to warrant a shootout with Jai Ferenhal?"

"I—" Zoey bowed her head and lowered her arms to her waist. "I don't know."

"*What?* What do you mean you *don't know?*" Perra lifted both arms into the air and gestured with open palms. "How can you not know? What if it's a bomb or something? Do you not ask questions?"

"Precious cargo, Perra." Zoey lifted a sour gaze. "It goes with the territory."

"It's a shift drive core," Ross said in Korish.

Zoey and Perra lowered stunned expressions to the floor where Ross sat at their feet.

"Beyond top secret, above high-military. We're talking the upper tiers of the Suth'ra Society." Ross cleared his throat and switched back to English. "That being said, we need to plot a course for Hollow Hold. If it isn't obvious by now, your recipient is dead." He turned and caught Max's stupefied expression from the bedchamber doorway. "Er, I mean ... meow, I'm a cat."

CHAPTER 10

Andromeda's vibrant colors poured through the transparent ceiling of the cargo bay. Zoey sulked in a plastic chair beside the bio-lock safe with her arms folded across her chest. She stared at a random crate across the room as restless fingers rapped upon her bicep. Perra leaned back on the far wall with her arms crossed behind her waist. Her wearied eyes studied the metal floor through a blank expression. Max stood in between them with one hand hooked on a cargo net, balancing himself as he surveyed the magnificent vista above. Ross sat upright in the chair opposite of Zoey with ears cocked back and brow lowered in what seemed like intense concentration, but in all likelihood amounted to little more than a strong desire to nap.

A ping on Zoey's comdev broke the dead silence. With a hesitant hand, she scooped the device from atop the safe and gave it an unwilling glance. A heavy sigh departed her lungs as she closed her eyes and lowered her head. She tossed the comdev back onto the safe, sending hollow clanks into the cargo bay. Leaning forward, she rubbed her temples before relaying the obvious news.

"Ross was right. Navashea is dead."

Perra plunked her head back onto a locker. Max raised an eyebrow and shifted puckered lips across his face, unsure of how to react. Ross shrugged in the exact way one would imagine a cat shrugging. As Zoey and Perra shouldered the weight of the casualty, Max turned to Ross and decided to clear the air.

"How did you even know about the package?"

"Remember Kenny at CounterPet?" Ross said. "Yeah, he was working with one of SSA Navashea's associates. Once word got out that the cargo was en route to Europa, they wanted to install a few inconspicuous ringers should things go south. So, they gave me all the information I needed. We just happened to arrive as things were southern bound. Course, these badass young ladies managed to blast their way through Jai Ferenhal's entire entourage." Ross winked at Perra, who responded with a smirk.

"*You* were a ringer?" Zoey said with a skeptical gaze.

"A watcher, mostly. Intelligence gathering and the like."

Zoey chuckled. "So a domestic cyborg feline is a Council of Loken informant."

"Hey, nobody expects the Spanish Inquisition," Ross said with a cocky tone.

"Furthermore," Zoey said, glaring at Ross, "how did they know that we were on our way to Europa? *We* didn't even know until days before. The entire jaunt was planned on a whim. And on top of everything, we always put an enormous amount of effort into keeping our ship off any and all radar. We're even invisible to high-military."

"Navashea had been tracking the package from the moment you took possession. They attached a beacon to the shift drive core. It—"

"Impossible," Perra said, shaking her head. "We would have found something like that on launch prep."

"Not this one," Ross said. "Low emission radiation, unique signature. Even high-military can't distinguish it from natural background radiation. Needless to say, Navashea was taking this very seriously."

"Sooo ..." Max said. "Navashea is dead. What does that mean?"

Zoey huffed and elevated an angered tone. "It means we don't have a damn drop. It also means that we don't get paid, that our reputation suffers, that we are stuck with hot cargo."

"Hot cargo?" Max said to Perra.

"Unclaimed high-value items," Perra said. "And given the nature of this item, we might as well be hauling lava."

Zoey snapped at Max. "It means, Earthman, that we are now the hunted."

Max cringed with what seemed like an appropriate level of concern, again unsure of how to respond.

"It also means that we have to listen to your fuzzball companion and make for Hollow Hold. We have to take this"—Zoey slammed an open palm down onto the safe—"to one of the most corrupt and anarchistic systems in the entire supercluster. So, there's that."

Max raised his hand with the enthusiasm of a first-grader. "I vote we don't do that."

"We don't have a choice," Ross said. "It's the best chance we have for contacting the Suth'ra Society."

* * *

If one were to describe the Suth'ra Society in a single word, it would have to be the most obscure synonym of bizarre. The entity existed not only as a collective of the most gifted scientific minds the universe had to offer, but also as a wasteland of social ineptitude. Asking a member of the Suth'ra Society how they were doing on any given day would require a group study lasting for several weeks to devise a satisfactory answer. Their culture endured as a means to a scientific end; nothing more, nothing less.

The curious story of their creation began thousands of millennia before Max hopped the multiverse. Two genius scientists working in a boring corner of a boring galaxy started what would become the Suth'ra Society. Their overall mission, to experiment without bother, was simple to an egregious fault.

When civilizations emerge, their architects have always been, and always will be, the smartest beings in a vast sea of stupid. The growing pains of building a good civilization entail convincing the stupid that the actions of the smart are worthwhile, often an exercise in futility. After all, morons hinder progress (and for the record, no truer statement has ever been uttered). And since stupid breeds like coked-up rabbits, it often mounts a devastating opposition. In most societies, the solution presents itself as a waiting game, where expanding generations of smarter beings await the inevitable die-off of their stubborn counterparts.

Dimwitted hamstringing will declare itself in countless ways, the most popular catalyst being slights on imaginary friends. As a notable example, the tiny dwarf planet of Burgadim spawned a primitive race known for its adamant resistance to change. A trip through the mind of a typical Burgadimian would yield the following proclamation: *I believe that everything in the universe was created for me by Babingobip, the toad-faced god of Finklemek. Smart beings say smart stuff that contradicts my overly simplistic views. I believe that offends Babingobip. Thus, I must resist smart beings to please Babingobip.* The entire race died off when a sudden shift in fertility rendered traditional reproductive methods ineffective. A visiting scientist from a neighboring planet discovered that a simple adjustment would save the species, but as the last Burgadimian said on his deathbed, "This is how we've always done it."

Enter Gleek and Qii, two gifted scientists who applied their superior intellects to the limitations of their own primitive society. As expected, they struggled with a predictable amount of resistance. However, Gleek and Qii were Minoparks, a unique humanoid species that enjoyed exceptionally long lifespans. Therefore, when the deficient majority of their species challenged the integrity of their research, they opted not to waste time on a social sway campaign. Instead, they disavowed their species and ventured into the ungoverned blackness of deep space where they could conduct their research without the interference of simpleminded dullards. Neither scientist set foot on soil again.

Afloat in their unconstrained superlab, Gleek and Qii indulged in every pure intellectual's fantasy: discovery for the sake of discovery. Curious questions found hard-lined answers without any obstruction whatsoever. As questions increased in difficulty, they decided to solicit the help of their fellow ostracized academics. After a while, the superlab had grown into a vibrant and awkward community of super-geeks doing super geeky things. The spiderweb of docked ships and pod components resembled the space equivalent of a massive multi-car pileup on a foggy interstate highway. The group dubbed themselves the Suth'ra Society because Jerry thought it sounded cool.

Years passed, then decades, then centuries, then millennia. The colossal dweeb station grew and grew, wandering about empty space with a destination of nowhere. Having no fixed coordinates of any kind, the nomadic society enjoyed an excessive level of secrecy. When recruiting new members, they relayed complex puzzles to potential candidates. Solving these near-impossible puzzles, a task only feasible for gifted prodigies relegated to the dark corners of social expulsion, revealed the temporary location of the roaming mega vessel. Soon thereafter, another ship docked itself to the hideous metal snowflake.

If a worthy candidate solved the puzzle and found the roaming vessel, they needed to recite the sacred pledge. After docking, a candidate stood before a senior Suth'ra recruiter. He, she, or it asked the candidate what area of study they intended to devote the rest of their life to. The candidate answered. The recruiter then asked *why*. The candidate then answered *why the bleep not?* (*Bleep* being the literal translation of *fuck* in Minoparkish.) The recruiter concluded the exchange by offering the candidate a high-five, or whatever number sufficed, before inviting them aboard to enjoy some refreshments. At that point, the candidate, now a Suth'ra member, spent the rest of their life aboard the vessel.

As millennia passed, the vast conglomerate organized itself into several sects devoted to specific areas of study. Every now and then, a sect broke off from the central hub and floated away, disappearing into their own aimless abyss. Before long, the Suth'ra Society had expanded to all corners of the universe, without a single traceable entity. Each misshapen metal flower possessed an array of sophisticated cloaking techniques, making them all but invisible to detection. And should a lucky passerby happen upon one, the structure would, in all likelihood, be dismissed as an abandoned trash heap.

The Suth'ra Society studied, tested, and discovered under the shrouds of space and time. But without a planet to protect or girls to impress, they simply blurted their peer-reviewed data out into the cosmos. Civilizations lucky enough to capture, translate, and apply Suth'ra signals have often found themselves liberated from conflict or destroyed altogether. Numerous societies have thrived and/or perished as a direct result of Suth'ra indifference. As the adage goes, if you give a kid a rock, he'll break a window. But if you give a kid a pocket-sized thermonuclear bomb with a trillion megaton yield, he'll destroy the world.

A humble theoretical physicist by the name of Rumac was a proud member of the Suth'ra Society. Like all members, Rumac carried the one simple name; a practice based not on rule, but rather on the unsaid understanding that learning family names and arduous pronunciations forced unwanted social interactions and wasted valuable brain space. Rumac was a crafty humanoid with a stocky build, deep-set eyes, leathery bronze skin, and a bushy white beard that reveled in its own wayward agenda. Hailing from a tiny moon orbiting a tiny planet inside a tiny galaxy, Rumac found himself obsessed with space travel. Most of his intellectual motivation came from an overwhelming need to break free of his tiny existence. He joined the Suth'ra Society in order to devote his remaining days to the study of hyperspace. His inquiries yielded sophisticated jump drive designs that powered the majority of space-faring vessels. But on one fateful day, he got a nutty idea.

Rumac was the father of the modern jump drive, the concept of hooking a distant particle with the concentrated power of a manufactured neutron star. Always wanting to improve on the concept, Rumac wondered what would happen if he could harness the power of a manufactured black hole. Assuming the drive would save a few valuable microseconds, he embarked on a mission to develop a core that could crush a clump of atoms even further to create a small black hole. And so, he did just that.

When it came time to test his device, he plucked one of the countless ships from the enormous docking web and installed the new drive core. When he activated the device and jumped to a new destination, his bushy beard and bald head had reversed themselves. The next jump corrected the problem, but the entire color spectrum had polarized itself. Curious fingers stroked his scraggly beard as he gazed into the open whiteness of space peppered with the black dots of stars. After a snort of concern, he initiated the next jump. A thankful smile greeted the visual correction, but inverted itself with the realization that he had lost his thumbs.

Jump after jump, Rumac marveled at the various tweaks to his own reality. While struggling to work the cockpit controls inside a five-dimensional world, the revelation dawned on him: he was jumping between parallel universes. The coordinates he entered, while accurate, ended up hooking their corresponding particles in adjacent universes. Hundreds of jumps and puzzled expressions later, he had returned to his own familiar universe. He redocked with the aimless Suth'ra station and uninstalled the drive core. Proud eyes and a gratified smile fell upon the silvery basketball in his hands. Rumac basked in the realization that he had become the very first being in all of existence to verify the multiverse. With a grunt of satisfaction, he tossed the device into the nearest airlock and gifted it to space, complete with an autograph and simple instructions for use. He then returned to his study to address the next question on his list.

The shift drive core floated in space for several years before landing on a derelict moon inside the Fornax Cluster where chance brought it into contact with a family of octopus-like tourists. Xarther Yithik, a doctor in training on the planet the moon orbited, along with his lovely spouse and various tentacled offspring, were enjoying some low-gravity bouncy fun on the moon's powdery surface. Ticalic, the oldest of his offspring, presented his father with a silvery round rock he had found. Xarther, unsure of what his son had brought him, studied the foreign writing upon its surface and made the determination that the object looked important enough to keep and deliver to a physicist friend.

Said friend, a nerdy octo-creature with stumpy tentacles and buggy eyes, consulted a language professional who deciphered the message. Gasps (well, more like gurgles) erupted as they realized what lay before them: a dangerous piece of Suth'ra technology. As a wise and peaceful race, the octo-creatures, known as Glurbiks, knew that the device needed protection under a veil of secrecy. Should a greedy maniac obtain such a device, they could plunder adjacent galaxies for power, wealth, and other personal gains. After much debate in the Glurbik Assembly, they decided to deliver the device to the Council of Loken, a peacekeeping faction located deep inside the Andromeda Galaxy. Their sector representative, Senior Security Advisor Verina Navashea, agreed to accept the device in confidence and shroud its whereabouts. With an official plan in motion, the final step was to secure delivery. All options considered, nothing came close to the reliability and reputation of the Precious Cargo Delivery Service. And considering the cargo, they spared no expense by requesting the best courier in the fleet. One name topped the list: Zoey Bryx, known in the black as The Omen.

*   *   *

"So what's Hollow Hold?" Max said.

All three of his travel companions turned to him and answered with irked stares.

"Oh c'mon, I've been off my own planet for less than ..." Max fished the comdev from his pocket and noticed that the location services had converted Earth time to universal pochs. "Hell, I have no idea now. What on Earth does this mean?" He pointed at an Artist-Formerly-Known-As-Prince-like symbol that followed a series of numbers.

"Well, *on* Earth it means nothing," Ross said.

Perra snickered.

Zoey huffed and shook her head. "You really are just a doltish infant."

Max pouted and lowered his comdev.

Zoey shot a sour gaze to Perra. "I still think we should just dump them at the nearest port."

"You know damn well we can't do that," Perra said in a level-headed tone. "By now, every crook in the Veiled Trader network knows our faces. *All* of our faces. Do you think that dumping an Earthling and his talking cat on some random rock wouldn't draw unwanted attention?"

Zoey maintained her glare, but sighed in agreement.

"They're part of this now," Perra said, glancing at Max and Ross.

Max slouched and sighed with a little too much drama. "Part of *what*? With all due respect, nobody has told me shit."

Zoey leapt from her chair and lunged for Max, causing the entire cabin to erupt in commotion. Perra darted forward and wrapped her hands around Zoey's waist, preventing the ensuing violence. Max scurried backwards and fell to the floor as Zoey's flailing arms collided with cargo boxes. Her clawing hands snagged netting as her gnashing teeth showered saliva and insults. Perra's planted feet squeaked across the cold metal floor as she struggled to subdue her lover's rage. Ross hissed from his chair a few times for good measure. With her dwindling strength, Perra jerked back on Zoey's torso, sending her tumbling to the floor.

"What has gotten into you?" Perra said, gesturing with open palms.

"He's going to get us all killed," Zoey said from the floor, pointing at Max. "You know it. I know it. Hell, I bet the cat even knows it."

"Yeah, sounds about right," Ross said with a straight face.

"What the hell, man?" Max said.

Zoey scrambled to her feet, prompting Perra to harden her stance.

"Hold on, ladies," Ross said with a swagger. "Let me handle this one." He leapt down from his chair, trotted over to Max, and hopped on the nearest cargo crate. With the temperament of a disappointed father, he stared at Max and took a deep breath. "Okay, listen. That safe over there contains the most dangerous thing in the universe. We have it. Bad people want it. Bad people will kill us to get it. The person that was supposed to take it and keep it safe has been killed by the bad people. Now we have to return it to those who created it, a group of unreachable weirdos, in hopes that they can destroy it without destroying the fabric of space and time. In order to do that, we have to infiltrate a hellish place known to harbor a few disgraced members of said group. That's Hollow Hold, a cave planet full of crazy people."

Max stared at Ross through glassy eyes. Perra and Zoey traded uneasy glances, expecting a sudden burst of hysteria. Ross cocked his ears back while maintaining eye contact with the catatonic orbs inside Max's skull. A tense silence filled the room, broken only by the dull hum of the main engines. Everyone remained still, awaiting the verdict.

"Thank you!" Max said, throwing his arms up into the air. "Was that so hard?" He lifted to his feet, dusted himself off, and turned his attention to Zoey. "Now if you will excuse me, I'm going to go find a place to throw up."

Retiring to the bedchamber, Max stumbled over to a non-bed corner of the room and proceeded to decorate it with a spray of vomit. He spent a solid four seconds trying to locate the hidden sink basin before wiping his mouth on his sleeve and shuffling over to the bed. He slammed face-first onto the mattress and passed out.

CHAPTER 11

To the average observer, Hollow Hold embodied a horror show of life's deepest and darkest secrets. Its planet-wide cave system housed a vast collection of the weirdest and scariest beings that the universe had to offer. Despite its infamous reputation as an anarchistic nightmare, residents considered it a sacred refuge, an extraordinary place where anybody could be anybody without the slightest threat of interference. As a result, tenants guarded the rock as if it still retained material value.

Hollow Hold's parent star, a red dwarf nicknamed Boarsh Kem (*Final Eye* in the local mishmash of dialects), floated along the outer reaches of the Andromeda Galaxy. It served as a hub for three rocky planets and a pair of gas giants. Hollow Hold, the second rocky planet, shared a few similarities with Earth, including size and orbital period. Its rusty red surface and countless black cave entrances gave it a menacing presence, like a bruised golf ball with a bad attitude. The atmosphere, with a comfortable 70/30 mix of nitrogen and oxygen, provided easy habitation for most humanoids. In addition, the planet contained ample fresh water and a myriad of red algae species, both surface and subterranean, hence the brickish hue.

First discovered by a mining colony, the unnamed planet teemed with precious metals. Over the course of several millennia, generations of miners stripped the planet bare and grew wealthy in the process. The operation created an enormous network of massive caves that stretched for hundreds of thousands of kilometers, many large enough for galactic cruisers to pass through. With excavation complete, the colony abandoned the hollowed husk and moved on to shinier pastures, leaving the planet with less than half of its original mass. For centuries, the planet floated around its tiny star like a gigantic sphere of Swiss cheese.

Then came the Argovar, one of the most infamous factions of organized crime in the entire supercluster. They stumbled upon the pockmarked planet and decided to use it as a new base of operations. As their organization grew, its members familiarized themselves with the colossal cave network. For decades, the Argovar amplified their nuisance throughout the galaxy, terrorizing every region from the independent outer arms to the peaceful inner core.

Before long, they caught the attention of the Council of Loken, a powerful peacekeeping conglomerate. Deciding to intervene, the Council devised a militarized plan aimed at eliminating the Argovar. They assembled a formidable assault fleet and descended upon the planet with hundreds of attack ships. However, the Argovar remained hidden inside the caves, refusing to surrender or fight in open space. The assault fleet entered the caverns, leaving a small cohort in orbit to prevent a retreat. The resulting battle devolved into a systematic slaughter in favor of the Argovar. Despite their inferior firepower, the Argovar used their extensive knowledge of the cave system to ambush Council ships at every nook and turn. The ships in orbit came under heavy fire from the cavern depths, rendering their retaliation tactics futile. A near-total loss, only two Council ships managed to escape into hyperspace, both with severe damage. To this day, the Battle of Hollow Hold remained the most devastating defeat for the Council of Loken. And from that day forward, the planet found itself immune to any and all forms of jurisdiction.

Word of the battle spread far and wide, cementing the planet's legendary status. The stronghold attracted unscrupulous beings from all over the supercluster, wanting nothing more than the freedom from control. The planet became a haven for countless criminal elements, all working out of its ominous caverns. Even seedy non-violent individuals sought shelter within its rocky walls. A large network of black markets emerged along with primitive housing and crude agriculture. The planet featured all the hallmarks of a budding civilization, but without a single native being. As time progressed, Hollow Hold became synonymous with lawless freedom.

Few things in the universe were as intimidating as entering the caves of Hollow Hold. Even before the tug of orbit, ships received a hostile barrage of security checks, in a manner of speaking. Should a vessel carry a governance beacon of any kind, missile turrets blew it out of the sky without the courtesy of a hello. Obtaining access depended on a chaotic examination of character (or lack thereof), none of which guaranteed entry. An inbound crew could lose their ship and their lives for something as trivial as an offensive paint color.

Once cleared for entry, a ship was free to enter and explore any cave they wanted. However, it paid to have a basic understanding of what sects dwelled where, as visiting ships could meet their demise by igniting a petty turf squabble. Most of the larger caves offered safe passage, as they harbored a diverse collection of residents and markets. In other words, they expected a constant flow of traffic, to a reasonable degree.

A thick spider web of steel support beams lined the tunnel walls from surface to core, creating a fibrous skeleton that kept the planet from imploding under the weight of its own gravity. Crude docking platforms littered the steel framing along with thousands of kilometers of grated metal panels, forming a welded mishmash of interconnected walkways. With no traffic directors of any kind, ships just picked an open dock and locked in manually.

The patchwork cave floors teemed with life around the clock. Shady merchants peddled their stolen wares from carts or derelict shacks. Rustic bars swelled with thirsty outlaws. Food vendors hawked exotic tastes with nothing forbidden and nothing disclosed, filling the tunnels with enticing yet somewhat offensive aromas.

Robed silhouettes shuffled around dim allies, making illicit deals in the open air without fear of repercussion. Dust and dirt adorned every public surface, giving the locale a grimy Old West vibe. A sleazy underlayer of tenacity served as an axiomatic foundation. Hollow Hold did not exist for the pleasure of dainty tourists. It was a reckless underworld where the strong thrived and the clever survived.

Most residents lived inside the middle core, deep enough to take advantage of predictable temperatures, yet far enough away to maintain privacy. Many tenants never ventured outside of the cave system, content to live out their lives in the dim recesses of service tunnels. Some dwellings offered a more polished feel with smooth stone surfaces, running water, and electricity. Others lived in the lower core, an area of filth and disrepair, the dark and primitive reaches that even residents dared not explore. The unwritten rule was this: know your knock, because it might be your last.

* * *

Max awoke as a six-legged eggplant with tentacle arms and the head of a praying mantis. He yelped (well, more like hiss-spit) and leapt out of his spongy moss bed. The jolt startled Ross, a giant fungal spore with spidery legs and a killer mullet. Max spun around his enclosure, a botanical garden box with bark walls and a grassy floor. He glanced up to find a ceiling of blinking red eyes staring back at him. He tried to scream, but ended up scorching the wall with a raging pillar of fire breath. With that, his brain tapped out. Max fainted and fell backwards onto the moss bed. Amused, Ross barfed up a banana peel.

* * *

Max awoke to a chorus of shrieking harpy dragons with baby legs and ...

* * *

Max awoke to a throbbing headache. The faint hum of the ship's engines within the walls soothed his psyche and confirmed his whereabouts; still in space, still on his way to a dreadful destination.

His troubled mind replayed the conversation from the previous day while tired eyes stared into the abyss. Despite the ongoing stress of the unknown, rousing in the void of space seemed much easier than stirring in his own familiar bed. A near-constant influx of new experience allowed his brain to let go of tedious burdens. In a strange sense, he had found peace among the chaos.

Lying on his side, he offered a smirk to the darkness while spooning a large, furry blanket. After a hearty sigh, Max decided to greet the new day with a fresh perspective and deal with whatever oddities it threw at him. First on the docket: his blanket's heartbeat.

"Oh, are you awake?" the blanket said.

"What the—" Max shoved his bed companion off the mattress and onto the floor.

"Denchi," the flustered floor blanket said, illuminating the room.

Max pressed his back to the rear wall and tossed an arm over his face, shielding his eyes from the sudden burst of light. A tiger-like humanoid with orange stripes lifted to its feet, dusted itself off, and turned to face a horrified Max.

"What the hell, man?" it said with a charming British accent.

"Wait ... Ross?"

Ross narrowed his eyelids. "No, your mum. Who else would I be?"

Max struggled to inject his sleepy brain with cognizant thought. "But you, uh ... you're, um ..." He closed his eyes to gather the ridiculous sentence. "You're a ThunderCat."

"A what?" Ross scrunched his furry humanoid brow. "You mean those weirdos in tights with the bat-signal sword?"

"Nevermind." Max applied a vigorous facepalm, then remembered his headache. After a grunt and grimace, he swung his legs out of bed and settled his bare feet onto the cold metal floor. Dropping his face into both hands, he proceeded to massage an aching scalp.

"Want me to get you something for that headache?" Ross said.

"Yeah, would you?"

"No. Get up and get it your bloody self."

"Dick."

"Prat." Ross hissed at Max and left the room.

"So that's my day," Max said under his breath. "I get to do battle with Lion-O."

"That's racist," Ross said from just outside the door.

Max rolled his eyes as he tossed the sheets aside and arose from the bed. His battered body lifted into a long stretch, unleashing an array of aromas that twisted his face in disgust. Realizing that he hadn't enjoyed a shower since the day before he left Earth, he stepped forward and studied the smooth black access panel on the wall. Pursing his lips to the side, he lifted a finger and placed a random tap upon the surface. A wall panel next to the bed slid open, revealing a compartment full of fresh linens. The panel closed with a subsequent tap. He selected another random location, which filled the room with a throbbing audible invasion that he could only assume was music. He speed-tapped the panel again, killing the vile noise. After a quick shiver, he moved his fingertip to a new position and cringed before tapping another mystery command. A lower drawer shot out into his shin, prompting a yawp of pain. "Bah! Mother of ferrets!" he said, cueing Perra to enter the room.

"Are you okay?" Perra said with concerned eyes.

"Obviously not," Max said, hunched over and rubbing his shin.

Perra smiled and patted his back. With a few quick taps, she reset the room to its default configuration. Panels slid shut, lights adjusted, and dirty sheets disappeared into a wall slot beside the bed.

"So what are you trying to do?" Perra said.

"Take a shower."

Perra glanced around the room. "Does it look like we have lavatory facilities on a tiny boat like this?"

Max shrugged, unsure of what to say.

"Here." Perra tapped on the upper right corner of the panel. A large section of the wall slid aside, revealing a moderate washbasin, a backlit mirror, and shelves of what resembled aerosol containers. She plucked a white canister from the shelf and handed it to Max. "This is your shower until we dock again. Just spray it on the problem areas. It'll do the rest." Perra winked at Max, then turned and left the room.

Max studied the container and noticed several lines of black and red symbols. "Well, here's hoping I don't do anything in red." He applied some spray to an armpit and awaited the results. An odd tingling sensation infected his skin and ended with the faint crackle of dissolution. He lowered a leery nose into his pit and raised his eyebrows in surprise. A swift hand wipe confirmed that all noticeable grime and aromas had vanished, leaving his skin smooth and moisturized. "Now that's just plain cool."

"It's a very effective blend," Perra said, poking her head around the corner. "It dissolves contaminants, kills bacteria, and seals the skin under a thin layer of antibiotic cream. Trust me, after a few pochs in the black, it becomes your best friend."

"I can see why. Thank you."

"You're welcome." Perra offered a chummy smile. "Oh, also, the green canister is for your face and the blue is for your mouth."

Perra ducked away, leaving Max to complete his body cleanse. He addressed all problem areas, fumbled his way through facial and dental hygiene, and wrapped up the session by teasing his hair into another lame style, even by Mulgawat standards. A cocky point-and-click at his own reflection completed the process. Spruced and rejuvenated, he slipped into a clean set of casual clothes and joined the group as they toiled in the cargo bay.

Ross sat upon a stack of cargo boxes with an outstretched leg hooked into cargo netting, providing the perfect lift for inner thigh licking (a startling image with an envious amount of limberness). At the rear of the cabin, Zoey tinkered with a shiny round device resting upon the opened bio-lock safe. An empty plastic box sat at her feet, along with a smattering of packing peanuts. Perra filled the adjacent seat with her hands tucked into her lap, studying Zoey's every move with an intense curiosity. Max continued his slow walk to the rear of the cabin, drawn by a meddling interest. With a final twist of her wrist, Zoey detached a small metal fixture from the round device.

"Got it," she said, holding the curved metal sliver in her hand.

"That's it?" Perra said.

"Yup." Zoey studied the crescent rod. "When you have this unique of a signature, it doesn't take much. Looks like a small core encased in aluminum." She handed the rod over to Perra, who twisted it around in her fingers.

"So this is the big bad, huh?" Max said, pointing to the silvery basketball.

"Indeed," Zoey said, slapping a hand onto its surface. "This is our imminent doom."

Max took his final steps forward and slipped his hands into his pockets, as if to avoid an awkward handshake with the device. With a slight bend of the waist, he caught his own distorted reflection in the metallic surface. His head and shoulders tilted from side to side, trying to get a read on the strange apparatus. Apart from panel lines and a handful of jack ports, the device resembled little more than a smooth silvery sphere, the same orbs that decorate tacky suburban gardens. Max frowned and wrinkled his forehead. "Hmm, I thought it would be more impressive."

"The inside is what counts," Perra said, twisting the device around to reveal several lines of etched lettering. "This is a rare form of Forliac. It says, *This device replaces a standard jump drive core and allows its host ship to visit parallel universes. Yes, they exist. Enjoy the great bag of marbles. With regards, Rumac of the Suth'ra Society.*"

"Hell, I could have told you that," Max said with a cocky tone.

Zoey and Perra glanced up at him with puzzled faces. An awkward silence fell upon the group, broken only by the sandpaper licks of Ross's grooming.

"Kidding. Bad joke."

Zoey lifted the shift drive core with both hands and lowered it back into the housing container. She topped it with the wayward peanuts, slid it back into the safe, and returned her gaze to Max. "Make no mistake about it, Earthman, the stakes in this particular game cannot be any higher." With a practiced motion, she closed the door to the safe and thumped an open palm onto its surface. The metal beneath her hand glowed for a moment before triggering a set of titanium locks. "When your moment comes, I need to know that you are with us to the end, no matter how horrific that end may be."

Max gulped and nodded. He filled his lungs, paused in contemplation, then expelled a whoosh of acceptance. "So what are we going to do?"

"The only thing we can do," Zoey said, rising to her feet. She snatched the tracking rod from atop the safe and shook it at Max. "We're going to dump this little bugger and plot a course for Hollow Hold." She gave him a cordial pat on the shoulder as she walked by. "Perra," she said, commanding her lover to attention. "I need you to get that dock remnant off the ship. Dispose of this while you're at it." She tossed the tracking rod to Perra, who snatched it out of the air with a deft hand.

"On it," Perra said, then refocused her attention onto spacesuit prep.

"Max," Zoey said.

Max jerked to attention like he knew from the movies; chin up, no eye contact, hip slap with rigid hands.

Zoey tilted her head, then shook it off. "We are going to a raging hellhole, so I need this place to reflect that reality. Hide the safe under a stack of random crates. Tear some netting, splatter some grease, do whatever you can to make the cargo bay look shoddy and disorganized. We need to look like a drifter ship on the off chance we get boarded."

"Yes sir, ma'am, sir," Max said, then dove into work.

"Ross," Zoey said, turning to the fuzzy humanoid.

Ross lifted his head from a full monty licking of his calf. His protruding tongue and ruffled brow conveyed an unacceptable level of imposition.

Zoey extended a finger as if to instruct, but retracted it and clenched her fist closed. "Just keep doing what you're doing."

"That was the plan," he said, returning his attention to a moistened calf.

"In the meantime, I will be in the cockpit plotting our course. I want to be outside the Boarsh Kem system in 50 marks, so let's get a move on." Zoey clapped her hands, then turned and disappeared into the cockpit corridor.

Max raised his hand.

"20 marks is about an hour," Ross said. "A poch is a little under a week."

"Thanks," Max said and lowered his arm.

"De nada," Ross said without breaking tongue stride.

* * *

Lord Essien's ominous cruiser hung in the blackness of space above Europa. Its cylindrical hull stretched over a hundred meters. A jagged bow filled with cannons, torpedo tubes, and various antennas jutted outward like a metal sea urchin. Sunken turrets lined the sides, creating shadowy stripes down the exterior frame. Three massive engines in a triangle formation adorned the stern, each emitting the deep red glow of idleness. Its stealthy black skin sliced through the vacuum of space, creating a ghost-like presence that promised death to any who gazed upon it.

Its interior housed a small army of purple-skinned Varokins dressed in simple black uniforms, dedicating every action to the whims of their overlord. Lord Essien loomed over the control bridge from an elevated platform, scanning the room with vigilant eyes. The command post contained an arched arrangement of control panels in multiple rows, with tireless minions manning each station. A constant stream of blips and chirps filled the domed room as drudges tended to the floating battleship. The curvature of Europa's stark white horizon poured through the massive panoramic viewport. With palms planted upon the steel railing, Lord Essien let out an impatient sigh while tapping the cold metal with her black fingernails. She lifted a hardened chin as the crackling static of a holographic transmission appeared over the bridge.

"Lord Essien," said the hologram image of Jai Ferenhal. A charcoal gray pilot suit accentuated his leafy green skin and yellow hair. "The Rippers are ready to depart."

"Good," Essien said with obvious impatience.

"I shall not fail you, my lord."

"I know you won't." She sneered as a bead of sweat rolled down Jai's cheek. "I don't care if you have to shake down every last cave dwelling rat in that cesspool of a planet. You bring me that package."

"Understood."

"And Jai ..." Her face twisted into a demented scowl. "Should you fail, I need not remind you of my methods."

Jai gulped.

With a wave of her arm, Lord Essien killed the hologram feed. She barked orders to a navigation minion who tapped a sequence of keys into the console. The massive cruiser pitched to the side, bringing a small fleet of a dozen Ripper ships into the viewport. Essien tightened her grip on the railing while glaring beneath a furrowed brow. Her silvery eyes pierced the fleet as they aligned to shared co-ordinates. Each ship retracted its tentacled arsenal, housing the most feared collection of assault weaponry in the cosmos. Slivers of purple light tore over each ship as they blinked to the Boarsh Kem system.

CHAPTER 12

The airlock door slid shut behind Perra as she entered the cargo bay, still wearing her form-fitting spacesuit. One hand steadied her tarnished helmet as the other unlatched it from the connector ring, unleashing a brief hiss of pressurized air. She lifted the helmet over her head, tasted the air with a deep inhale, and whipped her ponytail from side to side. Turning to a wall locker, she unhooked the latch and swung the door open. The flimsy metal banged the adjacent wall and reverberated as it bounced back and kissed her elbow. She plunked the helmet into an upper cubby and proceeded to unzip her spacesuit. The heavy synthetic leather fell from her shoulders and down to her thighs, exposing a few pieces of thin undergarments. Unsheathing each leg, she dropped her bare feet onto the chilled floor and shivered as the brisk air raised goosebumps on her creamy orange skin. She rolled up the spacesuit in her arms and stuffed the wad of material inside the locker before reassembling her mechanic garb. With a final latch of her black boots, she turned towards the cockpit. "Dock detached and tracking core discarded. We're clear."

"Excellent, great work," Zoey said. Her hands danced across the control panel with the grace of a fighter pilot. An array of pings, beeps, and muted flashes responded to her every touch. Exterior accent panels shifted from a charcoal black to a deep crimson. ID letterings changed. The beacon signal adjusted. "Max, how are you doing?"

Max lifted his grease-stained hands and studied the bay through blackened digits. A quick scan confirmed a filthy and disorganized mess. A smattering of mismatched crates lay in awkward piles. Frayed netting dangled from ceiling hooks and covered piles of rubbish. Grease stains adorned the walls in displeasing nonsensical patterns. Countless boot prints cut through a fresh layer of floor grime. A collection of dents, dings, and scrapes completed the illusion.

Max nodded and turned towards the cockpit. "The place looks like a post-kegger frat house."

Silence responded.

"It looks great," Perra said, patting Max on the back. "He did a good job."

"Excellent," Zoey said. "Thanks, Earthman. You may just prove useful yet."

"Don't get your hopes up," Ross said from a cozy pile in the bedchamber.

"Says the most useless member of the crew," Max said, poking his head around the door.

"Never claimed to be useful." Ross lifted his head and shot a glare at Max.

"Whatever, Garfield. You just sit there and enjoy the fruits of our labor."

"That's racist."

"Stop bickering, children," Zoey said, injecting a much-needed dose of amusement. "I will pull this freighter over and give you what for."

Perra snickered as she assumed the co-pilot chair next to Zoey.

"That should be everything, no?" Zoey said.

"Yup, as far as I can tell," Perra said, strapping herself into the chair. "Did you get a good course plotted?"

"I believe so, yes. Well, in a sense. I did what I could with limited information. Boarsh Kem seems to go out of its way to remain cryptic." Zoey sighed and pulled up a crude hologram of the planetary system. "I should be able to put us just outside the third's orbit. From there, we can make a cautious approach and gauge responses accordingly."

Perra pursed her lips and studied the rotating hologram. Zoey leaned back in her seat and gazed out the viewport with a vacant expression, her fingertips rapping atop the control panel. Perra reached over and gripped her hand, silencing the taps. They squeezed each other in a moment of solidarity. Zoey bowed her head and closed her eyes, trying to combat an obvious and weighted anxiety. Perra offered a hopeful smile.

"You have always managed to pull us through difficult and dangerous situations. I am beyond confident that you will get us through this one."

Zoey nodded, her crumpled face radiating doubt. "I wish it were only dangerous. We can handle danger. Hell, we *thrive* in danger. But this ..." She lifted her head and turned watering eyes to Perra. "This is suicidal."

Perra paused at the sight of her shaken lover, her rock, The Omen of the black sea. With a gentle hand, she opened their palms and interlocked fingers with her best friend. "Then so be it. How often do you get to put everything on the line for the right reasons? We're doing exactly that, for the good of everyone, in every corner of every universe, and I will be right there by your side until the end."

A quivering smile crept up Zoey's cheek. "I love you so much."

"And I love you, my sweet."

Zoey kissed the top of Perra's hand. She expelled a few hasty breaths and wiped her watering eyes, trying to shake off the mounting pessimism. With a forced confidence, she input the jump coordinates and turned to the cargo bay with a stern voice. "Anyone not strapped down in 20 ticks will have a very unpleasant ride."

Ross raised an eyebrow in casual acknowledgment, then flipped over in the bed facing the wall. His long prehensile tail wrapped itself around a leg post. A panicked Max raced inside the bedchamber and lunged for the control panel. His extended finger stopped just before tapping the smooth black surface, realizing at the last second that he had no idea what he was looking for. Frantic eyes darted around the room as shoe soles squeaked across the metal floor like a frightened basketball player.

"Garpa dreka," Ross said, commanding a seat bottom to lower itself from the wall, complete with straps and a plush cushion.

"Thanks, buddy," Max said as he plopped himself onto the seat. He looped the straps over his shoulders and sighed with relief as he fastened the final buckle.

"De nada," Ross said, still facing the rear wall.

A large green icon pulsed on the control panel, painting Zoey and Perra's hesitant faces with every beat. A hush fell upon the cockpit as both Mulgawats stared at the icon. Zoey turned to Perra and offered a half-smile of acceptance. "Are you ready?"

"Not in the slightest."

"Me neither."

Zoey slapped a palm down on the glowing icon. Perra closed her eyes and clutched her armrests. The winding build of the jump drive filled the cabin and climaxed with a sliver of purple light.

* * *

Jai's Ripper ship loomed over the rusty red surface of Hollow Hold, floating in upper orbit like a mechanical squid stalking prey. Its large central engine glowed with the deep red of idleness as beacon scanners surveyed the incoming traffic. An endless flow of derelict vessels blinked in and out of the system at random intervals. Each hasty exit maddened the scanning AI, resulting in numerous buzzes of failed ID acquisition. With no discernible form of traffic control, locating a specific ship in the Boarsh Kem system proved as difficult as finding a jarvy in a harmenash (the local equivalent of a needle in a haystack; the rough translation being a phallic vegetable in a dildo factory).

The deep purple glow of the Ripper's angular console traced Jai's hardened expression. Impatient fingers tapped on the sleek control panel, sending hollow clinks through the drab yet sophisticated cockpit. The sharp edges of gunmetal plating accented his chiseled jaw. A hologram of planetary traffic hovered above the console, bathing his skin in a warm yellow glow. Squinting eyes scrutinized the patchwork ships as they entered and exited orbit. Beacon scanners pinged in the background with every new arrival, covering a radius of several hundred gamuts.

The spidery shadow of a minion Ripper caught Jai's attention as it sped towards him from below the horizon. His eyelids blinked with the cold indifference of a drunken sloth on antidepressants. The ship halted its approach about 50 meters away, cueing the crackling static of an incoming hologram transmission. Jai shifted his focus to the glowing green image of the minion pilot, a welcome reprieve from the incessant pings of background scanners.

"Master Jai," the image said in a hissing voice. "A potential target has just appeared outside of the Zuzax orbit."

"Send me the details," Jai said with a flattened tone. A transparent panel of data figures appeared in bright yellow type beside the hologram image. His eyes narrowed as he leaned forward to study the information. "Go check it out."

"At once, sir," the minion said, then disappeared in a wash of static.

The minion Ripper about-faced and sped away with a burst of white light. Jai turned away and grimaced as the faint rumbles of departure crept around the cabin. He sneered at the blackness of space as the ship faded into the distance. With a restless sigh, he returned his attention to the planetary traffic.

* * *

"Ripper inbound!" Zoey's frantic hands danced across the control panel, prepping for battle.

"Hailing or assault bound?" Perra said, double-checking the statuses of critical systems.

"Don't know yet. There's only one ship and it's in no particular hurry, so I assume they don't recognize us. Probably a scout."

Perra flicked a series of overhead switches, then returned her attention to the viewport. "Jump is spun if we need it. All cannons and missiles online."

"Good," Zoey said, gripping the control yoke. "It's showtime."

Ross sauntered into the cockpit, munching on a piece of mystery fruit. Casual eyes brushed over the pulsing control panel before leaning forward to peer out the viewport. His complete lack of concern sucked the intensity from the room. Zoey and Perra traded puzzled expressions as Ross took another bite of fruit and let out a satisfied grunt. "Take everything offline," he said.

Zoey whipped a startled gaze to the fuzzy humanoid. "*What?* You did hear me say 'Ripper inbound,' did you not? Eager to meet your furry creator?"

Perra responded with a cheek spasm.

Ross shrugged and maintained his even-toned demand. Gazing into the black, he lifted his brow and smirked as the Ripper continued its approach. "Jai knows you, does he not? He knows your weaponry, he knows your tactics, he knows your maneuvers. At this point, you might as well paint the ship orange and bark 'The Omen' through the beacon. Just saying." He took another bite of the crunchy green fruit.

Perra clenched her lips and returned her eyes to the console. Zoey's angered expression melted into a worried gaze. Her head shot back to the viewport as her racing mind struggled to process the obvious verdict. Ross dropped an elbow onto Perra's headrest and leaned for comfort.

"Shit," Zoey said. "Okay. Perra, spin everything back down, jump drive too."

"What?! What if we need to—"

"Perra! No time! Everything down. Leave a single ion cannon online."

Perra's horrified expression added twitching eyes and fluttering breaths as she disabled all drives and weapon systems, down to an ion cannon. "Done. I really hope you know what you're doing."

Zoey glanced up at Ross, who winked with a cool confidence.

Static erupted from a com speaker overhead, pushing a hissing voice into the cockpit. "Freighter vessel GXR-5442," the voice said in a mishmash of local dialects. "State the purpose of your presence."

"Target the Ripper," Ross said.

Zoey and Perra responded with whipping necks affixed to stunned faces.

"Are you insane?!" Zoey said, throwing her palms into the air.

"What she said!" Perra said, pointing at Zoey.

"Trust a kitty," Ross said, maintaining a calm demeanor. He took another bite of fruit and nodded with delicious approval.

Perra lowered her widened eyes to Zoey, who shook her head in disbelief.

"I repeat, state the purpose of your presence," the com voice said. "I will not ask again. Your destruction shall receive no warning."

Zoey huffed. "Well, today's as good as any to die."

With a hesitant hand, she tapped a sequence of keys, resulting in a ping of target acquisition. The small freighter tilted its stern towards the Ripper as crosshairs aligned in the viewport. Perra buried her face into her hands.

"What's going on?" Max said, poking his head into the cockpit.

"Your damn cat is about to get us all killed," Perra said into her shaking palms.

Max caught a glimpse of the Ripper in the viewport, cueing his eyelids to disappear into the back of his skull. Unable to speak in a coherent manner, he lifted a shaking finger and pointed at the spidery vessel. A quivering lip conveyed a healthy amount of terror.

"I am doing nothing of the sort," Ross said with a measured amount of sternness. He shot a sour gaze at Perra. "Everything is fine, just chill."

A warning siren buzzed around the cockpit as the Ripper responded with a targeting sequence of its own. Its ominous tentacles expanded into the blackness, silhouetted by the red glow of the rear engines. Strips of arming lights crawled up the arms, creating a burning flower of death.

"Disengage and establish com transmission," Ross said.

Without question, Zoey tapped her way across the control panel, killing the targeting sequence and backing down from the assault. A few more taps bridged a comlink. She gave a thumbs-up to Ross, who erupted with a barrage of unintelligible hisses and screeches. Zoey, Perra, and Max traded bewildered expressions. Ross raised a single finger, motioning for silence.

"Say again, freighter vess—" the static voice said, only to be interrupted by another barrage of hisses and screeches.

Ross motioned to kill the transmission, to which Zoey complied.

Both ships floated in the emptiness of space, facing each other, the Ripper locked for combat, the freighter a helpless target. Zoey, Perra, and Max held their collective breath, their eyes fixated on the pulsing arms of the Ripper. Ross munched away on his dwindling piece of fruit, as if to shun the imminent doom altogether. Then silence. The targeting siren ceased, leaving them to the comforting hum of the main engines. The pulsing red glow of the Ripper's readied arsenal faded to black. Its tendrils retracted as the vessel disengaged and faced the way it came. With a burst of white light, it leapt away from the immediate area and sped towards Hollow Hold.

All non-felines emptied their lungs of pent-up air. Perra plunked her forehead onto the console, resulting in a few blips of system errors. Zoey fell backwards into her chair and sank into the cushions with a newfound limpness. Ross watched with a near disinterest as the red glow of the Ripper faded into the distance. Max, still frozen in fear, turned his dried-out eyes to Ross.

"What the fucking fuck was that?!" Max said.

"That"—Ross tossed a nod to the viewport—"was me saving your arses."

Max's face twisted into an array of colorful expressions, none of which conveyed an understanding.

Ross patted Max's shoulder. "Careful now, don't hurt yourself."

"He's right," Zoey said, still lying across her chair like a crime scene victim. "He did save us. I, on the other hand, would have killed us all." Zoey took a deep breath and resumed a reasonable sitting position. "Like he said, they're looking for us. And in a place like this, things like training and caution stick out."

"Hence the batshit crazy display of complete and total stupidity," Ross said as he dropped the fruit core into a nearby incinerator bin.

"Smart," Zoey said, extending an open hand to Ross. "Very, very smart."

Ross grinned and grasped her hand. "Thanks." He lifted his gaze to the viewport and chuckled. "Oh to have been a fly on the wall in that Ripper cockpit."

*   *   *

The minion Ripper returned to Hollow Hold's upper orbit where Jai floated in the black. He eyed the ship with a dubious stare as it slowed into position, cueing the crackling static of a hologram transmission. The minion's bust pieced itself together in front of the viewport.

"Negative, Master Jai," the glowing minion said.

"Are you certain?" Jai said in a low, skeptical tone.

"Yes, Master. Same ship class, but different plating and components. They targeted me with an ionic blaster, but soon remedied their mistake." The minion snorted. "No advanced weaponry, no radiation signature. Just a drifter ship with a savage crew, most likely a thieving cohort, illegal salvage at best."

Jai maintained his unimpressed stare as he plunked a meaty hand upon the console, killing the transmission. The minion Ripper dropped from view and continued its methodical survey of planetary traffic. Jai sighed and turned his attention to a snack pack.

CHAPTER 13

Max and Ross stood in silence over the shoulders of Zoey and Perra as they guided the tiny freighter through an ocean of erratic traffic. Perra gnawed on her lower lip while adjusting the beacon output of a disguised presence. Zoey maintained a composed stare as she maneuvered the vessel around lumbering cruisers and patchwork fighters, trying to avoid any unwanted attention. The boxy ship seemed right at home among its battered brethren. An ashen cloud of tarnished hulls littered Hollow Hold's orbit, forming a conglomerate of shoddy repairs and battle scars; mere trash to the untrained eye, but a thriving cohort to the local population.

Hunks of twisted metal floated by the viewport, pulling Max's dangling chin along with them. "Are you sure none of these are looking to pick a fight?"

"I'm pretty sure *most* of them are looking to pick a fight," Zoey said.

"So, we're *not* safe after Ross's confrontation?"

"You can pretty much drop *safe* from your vocabulary at this point. He bought us an entrance pass and nothing more. Any one of these bastards could attack us at any time for any reason. Our best chance for survival is to *not* give them a reason." Her matter-of-fact words struck Max as somewhat comforting. "Speaking of which," she said, turning to Perra, "we need to load up some language."

Perra nodded and reached into a side compartment, retrieving the cylindrical language infuser. "Let's see what we got." She consulted the control panel for local dialects, then huffed and slumped in her seat. "Well then, only 3,384 unique languages are spoken in this system, not counting idioms."

Zoey raised an eyebrow. "Seriously?"

"Yes, unfortunately. We have to remember that every inhabitant here is some form of immigrant. And on top of that, the languages tend to blend. We can't exactly infuse ourselves with local nuance, so we are going to sound like newcomers no matter what."

Zoey sighed. "Fine. I guess we'll just have to wing it. Let's keep it simple and load up the majors."

"Agreed." Perra entered some filtering commands and studied the results. "I think we can get away with the top eight. From there it's a sharp decline in usage. The bottom 1,500 languages are spoken by less than five beings per."

"Eight it is then." Zoey turned her attention to Max and Ross while Perra loaded the infuser. "We will continue to speak English among ourselves. It's highly unlikely that anyone here will be able to eavesdrop on an Earth-tongue conversation."

"Well, considering I only speak English, that will be—" Max said before Perra thrust the infuser at him.

"Put this to your temple and press the red button," she said like an impatient mother.

Max grasped the metal cylinder with a reluctant hand. Flipping it into an open palm, he studied the foreign object with the curiosity of an awestruck toddler. He rolled the device back and forth and poked at it with his fingertips.

"Oh for pity's sake," Perra said and snatched the device from his hand. She stood from her chair, cupped his cheek, and planted the business end of the cylinder to his temple. Her annoyed face kept him from panicking as she pressed the red button, sending a jolt of data into his brain. Max's eyelids twitched as if contacts had rolled up into his sockets. After a few unsettling moments, he expelled a cache of air and turned a solemn gaze to Ross.

"I know Kung Fu," Max said in his best Neo voice.

"Ha, nicely done," Ross said.

They bumped fists like cocky jocks.

"Now say it in Bunt'a Ley."

"Ark con yem Kung Fu," Max said, stretching his face into a toothy smile.

"Wait," Perra said and glared up at Ross. "You already know Bunt'a Ley?"

"Yup. Kenny hooked me up. I got all of Virgo's greatest hits. I can even speak a rare dialect of sentient salamander." Ross gurgled with the throaty chant of a randy toad.

"That's quite enough," Zoey said, trying to focus on her approach.

Ross cleared his throat and smirked at Perra. She let out a polite snicker before raising the infuser to her own head and shooting a bundle of languages into her cranium. After a brief shiver, she passed the infuser to Zoey, who repeated the process and tossed it back to Perra.

The curve of Hollow Hold's rusty horizon filled the viewport as the group looked on with a nervous fascination. Streaks of light pierced the hazy green bubble as ships entered and exited the atmosphere. The control panel pinged and backlit itself with a pleasant shade of blue, signaling the encroaching barrier. Zoey pitched the nose of the freighter upward in preparation for an onslaught of turbulence. An eruption of creaks and clanks bounced around the interior as the vessel rumbled with entry. Max and Ross grasped the thick metal bars above their heads for balance. A bright orange glow enveloped the hull, spilling violent flames over the viewport. Zoey unclenched a hand from the yoke to input some stabilization commands.

"We'll be out of this in a few ticks," she said in a loud, vibrating voice. "The atmosphere here is pretty thin."

A few ticks later, the turbulence ceased, leaving them to the dull hum of the main engines. The orange glow of entry dissipated from the viewport, replaced by the grayish-green hue of a strange new atmosphere. Dark nimbus clouds reflected the red glow of the dwarf star hanging in the sky. Long columns of precipitation evaporated before reaching an endless sea of cavern entrances. Boundless stretches of razor-edged mountains snaked their way across the harsh landscape, serving as geological divides between shadowy caves. Glistening lakes of algae-laden water peppered the terrain, absorbing starlight into their red-green surfaces. All four newcomers drank the contrasted landscape through boggled eyes.

Perra broke the silence with a gasp of stupefaction. "For such a perilous place, it's actually quite beautif—"

Screams filled the cabin as a giant wall of metal sped past the viewport, ending in the fiery blaze of four massive engines. A thunderous wake engulfed the ship and jumbled the cargo bay, not that it mattered. Zoey and Perra jostled in their seats while Ross clung to the overhead bars for dear life. The sudden jolt knocked Max to the floor. His flailing hand nabbed one of Zoey's seat straps, preventing him from tumbling down the corridor. The rumbles stopped with an abrupt silence, allowing the screaming to follow suit. Zoey loosened her death grip on the yoke in order to stabilize the vessel. Perra gasped for breath with both hands atop her chest. Ross retracted his claws and dropped himself to the floor. After a grumble of irritation, he started pawing his poofed fur back into place. Max struggled to his feet while rubbing an aching neck.

"Everyone okay?" Zoey said.

Perra nodded and took a deep breath.

"Six lives left," Ross said.

"I may need a change of underwear," Max said. "But otherwise okay."

"Good," Zoey said. "Let's pick a cave and get out of this crazy sky."

"What about that one?" Perra said, pointing to a colossal cave entrance up towards the horizon. "Lots of steady traffic, probably a main port. Might be a good place to dock and look around."

"Works for me," Zoey said. "The sooner we're on the ground, the better."

Zoey slid an open palm up the control panel, igniting the main engines into full thrust. The freighter kicked forward and sped towards the distant cave entrance. Zoey's steady hands guided the tiny ship over mountain passes, careful not to venture over the open mouths of caves. Perra scanned the darkened depths with an astute gaze, studying their alloy skeletons and various docking patterns. An endless variety of dim lights speckled the interiors. Some formed obvious shapes, like the outlines of landing pads. Others appeared random at best, forming mysterious factions along the stony faces. Some even moved, as if giving chase like a dog to a passing car. Mangled bodies of metal lifted from the shadows and departed for parts unknown. Others sank into their respective abysses, bound for secret havens.

Cresting a final mountain peak, the ship found itself floating above a vast blackened sea accented by countless dots of light. Still cruising at an elevated speed, the tiny freighter seemed to hang motionless over the gargantuan cave mouth. Vessels of all shapes and sizes darted in every direction with no perceivable traffic pattern, like bees swarming around a hive. Zoey swiped her palm across the control panel, reducing speed and beginning a slow descent. A sinister shadow consumed the freighter as the waning sun disappeared behind a distant cave rim. Perra powered the external lights while Zoey steadied the hull thrusters. As their eyes adjusted to the dim light, a spiderweb of metal emerged. An enormous skeleton of steel pipes and girders twisted around each other and drove themselves into the jagged rock face. Grated walkways snaked around the mangled support structure and disappeared into pedestrian tunnels. Bright neon signs denoted various forms of business from bars and eats to goods and repairs.

An assortment of landing pads and docking stations jutted out from the internal framing. A complete lack of any meaningful regulation meant that some docks appeared safer than others. After descending several kilometers into the planet's interior, Perra spotted an empty landing pad devoid of any questionable construction. Zoey maneuvered the craft into position, engaging its three landing claws. The ship came to a rest upon the platform, resulting in a small thump of floor pressure. Zoey and Perra danced their fingers across the control panel, securing the ship and silencing the beacon. They unbuckled their harnesses as the main engines spun down.

Zoey tromped her way to the cargo bay, compelling Max and Ross to follow. She unlatched a cargo crate and sifted through its contents. Perra emerged from the cockpit and hooked her hand on a ratty cargo net. Zoey tossed a wad of fabric to each member. They unfolded grimy leather cloaks, complete with hoods, face wraps, and tarnished latches.

"Put those on," she said while slipping into her own.

The group complied without question.

Zoey hooked a final clasp and rolled her shoulders to loosen the fabric. "We have to assume that the Veiled Trader network knows who we are. Several are known to occupy Hollow Hold, so stay vigilant. Do not engage unless you have to. We keep our faces and colors hidden, enough to look threatening, but not overly suspicious. Group dress is not uncommon here as it denotes packs and sects, so our similarities shouldn't raise any eyebrows."

"What if we get separated?" Max said as he tightened a waist latch.

Zoey thought for a moment. "I would highly advise *not* getting separated."

Max turned to Ross, who shrugged in response.

Zoey unlatched a wall locker and retrieved two plasma pistols. She handed one to Perra and clipped the other to a belt underneath her cloak. Perra repeated the process. Max caught a glimpse of the weapons before they disappeared beneath leather flaps. Their stout and smoky bodies hung with the obvious weight of dense metal, much more robust than the compact versions he stared down on Europa.

"Nothing for us?" Max said, using the pitiful voice of a shunned child.

Zoey glared at Max. "I am not about to put a military-grade plasma weapon into the hands of an Earthling. I value my life and intend to keep it."

"Just stick close to us," Perra said, patting Max on the shoulder.

He glanced over to Ross for sympathy.

Ross lifted his furry hands, flexed talon-like claws from the tips, winked, then retracted them.

"Great," Max said, tossing his hood over his head. "Just a squishy, unarmed human on a planet full of intergalactic thugs. This should go well."

A few metallic thunks echoed from the airlock, followed by a mishmash of unintelligible grumbles. Zoey raised a fist into the air, silencing the room. Her eyes darted around the cargo bay, making sure that everyone and everything looked the part. She approached the airlock and paused to address the group with a lowered voice.

"Nobody says a damn word. Let me do the talking."

The group nodded as another round of thunks infected the room, this time a bit harsher in tone. Muted grumbles elevated to impatient bellows. Zoey tapped an adjacent wall panel, revealing a large, bulbous figure standing outside.

"He's alone. Don't do anything rash unless I do it first." Zoey armed the plasma pistol under her cloak, took a deep breath, then tapped the lower corner of the panel, opening the airlock.

She met eyes with a plump and perturbed creature that resembled a humanoid walrus. Tattered fabric stretched across rolls of exposed blubber. Roped suspenders and a thick leather belt struggled to hoist a pair of baggy brown pants. A pair of tusks protruded from a set of beefy jowls, one broken, and the other ground to a nub. Yellow eyes bulged atop a bed of scruffy whiskers. Beads of flop sweat rolled down a splotchy bald scalp. Zoey's puckered expression conveyed a combination of nasal and visual shock.

"Ye best have a capital reason for dropping yer vessel onto *my* flat," the bipedal walrus said.

His graveled voice sounded an awful lot like an Earth pirate caricature, causing Max to snort with amusement. The walrus shot him a death stare. Max used the opportunity to study the ceiling.

"Hey," Zoey said, snapping her fingers in front of the chubby face. "You talk to me. I'm the captain of this ship."

"Ship?" the walrus said, taking a laborious step inside. "You call this filthy coffin a ship?" His bloodshot eyes gave a quick scan of the cargo bay. "Looks more like a squatter box with meat warmers strapped to the back."

Zoey quashed Perra's obvious offense with a subtle hand gesture. Max continued his intimate study of the ceiling as the bumbling visitor lobbed skeptical gazes at each member of the crew. Ross winked at the smelly guest, resulting in a huff of indifference that sent ripples down rows of neck fat.

"You say this is your landing pad?" Zoey said, regaining his attention.

"Aye," the walrus said before spitting on the floor. "This be mine. And it comes with a usage fee."

"How much?"

The walrus stepped forward, causing the metal floor to whine beneath his feet. A drop of his unkempt chin brought him face-to-face with Zoey. "1,000 credits, per day."

Zoey smirked, then reached over and tapped the wall panel, closing the airlock. The walrus's eyes shifted from side to side in their sunken sockets. Zoey's gaze hardened, drawing a gulp from the uninvited visitor.

"How stupid do you think I am?" Zoey said, then drove the heel of her boot into the side of his knee.

The walrus yelped and began to fall. Zoey hooked his shoulder and slammed his back into the metal floor. A rush of air fled his lungs as a wave of impact echoed through the cargo bay. She drove a knee into his chest, unlatched her plasma pistol, and jammed the barrel underneath his chin.

"So that's your play? New ship comes to port and you shake them down for easy credits?"

He whimpered beneath a quivering chin.

"What's your name?"

"Da—Dork."

"*Dork?*" Max said with a hearty chuckle. "Your name is *Dork?*"

Everyone, including Dork, turned to Max with mirrored expressions of confusion.

"I don't get it," Ross said with a flat tone.

"How do *you* not get it?" Max said.

"I don't see the relevance."

"What? This is like, Earth insults 101. Dork. You know, whale penis."

"Enough!" Zoey said, killing the conversation.

Ross slapped Max in the back of the head while Perra dropped hers in embarrassment.

"Anyway, Dork," Zoey said, returning to the blubber beneath her knee. "I'm going to make a deal with you. Your life, for information. With me so far?"

Dork nodded like a terrified child.

"I'm going to ask you a few questions and you are going to answer. If I don't like the answer, or if one of my associates detects a lie, then I'm going to repaint these walls with that squish ball you call a brain. Understand?"

Dork nodded.

"Good. First question. Are you familiar with the Suth'ra Society?"

Dork nodded.

"Are you aware that a few of its disgraced members live inside these caves?"

Dork nodded.

"Do you know who or where they are?"

Dork paused for a moment, then shook his head.

"He's lying," Perra said and unlatched her plasma gun.

"No! No I'm not!" Dork squirmed beneath Zoey's knee. "I know they are here, but I know not who they are or where they hide. I swear. Please! Please do not kill me!"

Zoey slapped Dork across the face, silencing his weeping and writhing. She turned an open palm to Perra as if to thwart an impending assault. Perra stopped her approach and heaved, playing the bloodthirsty assassin to perfection.

"Final question," Zoey said, piercing Dork's watering eyes with a menacing gaze. "If *you* don't know ... do you know of someone who *does*?"

Dork closed his eyes, then nodded.

CHAPTER 14

Dork stood outside of the tiny freighter with his eyes lowered to the dusty platform. His plump fingers crawled over one another as jitters continued to erode any remaining composure. Ross stood beside him with claws exposed, staring at him like a hungry predator. Dork, shackled by an obvious cowardice, went out of his way to eschew eye contact. Amused by the palpable anxiety, Ross grunted and smacked his lips in order to prod the nerves of his prisoner.

Max, on the other hand, could not contain his outright distaste for the pungent air. A potent mixture of exhaust, excretion, and rotting meat assaulted his nose from every direction. Hacks and coughs filled his leathery facemask with every gust of wind. He tried to distract his mind by scouring the massive tunnel for anything interesting. Lifting his eyes to the sun-drenched hole far above, he studied the shadows of spaceships as they sailed across the greenish plane. Beneath the rim, he traced a winding path through tangled mazes of floodlights and flickering neon. Roaring thrusters, rattling pipes, and fervent residents combined to create a harsh atmosphere that made death metal concerts seem tame by comparison. Hollow Hold was alive in every sense of the word, using a caustic voice to spew its acidic breath.

Back inside the ship, Zoey shoved a final crate aside to reveal the bio-lock safe. She pressed an open palm to the surface, prompting a scanner to glow beneath her skin. The titanium bolts unlocked with muted thunks. She unlatched the door, swung it open, and yanked a plastic box onto the floor. Packing peanuts fell to the ground as she lifted the shift drive core from the container. Its shimmering surface reflected light around the room like a disco ball of doom. Perra kneeled beside her, scooped the wayward peanuts back into the box, and returned it to the safe. Zoey stared at her own reflection in the drive core, her eyes ambivalent as Perra's reflection merged into hers.

"You okay, my love?" Perra said.

Zoey sighed and shook her head. "This damn thing ... ruined our vacation."

They both shared a laugh as a much-needed moment of levity.

"Well, this place does have its charms," Perra said. "The locals are vibrant and I hear the red algae water is somewhat tolerable."

Zoey chuckled. "We will have to acquire a few bottles at the Hollow Hold gift shop."

She wrapped the shift drive core inside a greasy towel and lowered it into a frayed sling pack. Wads of tattered cloth and a handful of random machining parts served as cover. She tossed the strap over her shoulder and lifted to her feet. Perra followed her up and adjusted her cloak. A casual kick and slap shuttered the safe. They restacked the cover crates before turning to the airlock.

"You ready for this?" Zoey said.

"Nope, but let's do it anyway."

Perra took Zoey's hand and guided their bodies into a loving embrace. They squeezed each other in the middle of the cargo bay, drawing moans of contentment.

Perra offered a cheeky smile as she pulled away. "For what it's worth, this has definitely been the most interesting trip we have ever taken."

Zoey smirked. "Smartass." She hooked her arm around Perra's neck and kissed her on the forehead.

Perra wrapped her arm around the small of Zoey's back as they trudged towards the airlock. Boots clanked in unison atop the metal floor, sounding off a potential death march. They butted heads in a grave moment of companionship.

"Great job with Dork, by the way," Perra said. "I'm surprised he didn't soil his pants, not that we could tell."

"Couldn't have done it without you, my sweet. You play a masterful bad cop."

"Thanks, love." Perra sighed and flipped the cloak hood over her head. "Speaking of which, back into character."

Zoey adjusted the sling pack before tapping the control panel, reopening the airlock. A whoosh of rancid air poured into the cargo bay, causing both to flinch with disgust. Dork lifted his gaze to the hooded Mulgawats as they stepped outside the ship and onto the gritty landing pad. The airlock resealed itself with a thump of pressure. The grumbles of passing ships shook the platform, serving to highlight the ever-present danger of their surroundings. Perra paused to consult her comdev while Zoey continued her deliberate stride towards their rotund captive. Dork gulped as she took her final steps, bringing them face-to-face once again. Zoey's hood and mask fluttered in the noxious wind, amplifying her coldhearted stare. Ross seemed content to groom his forearm while Max continued his rigorous study of anything distracting.

"Orantha Nifan," Perra said, reading the output of her comdev. Her voice hiked a few decibels to combat the roaring environment. "Also known as The Dossier. She did multiple stints at the Mavcore Stockade for blackmail. She has a massive rap sheet, no surprise there. Mostly crimes pertaining to information trafficking. She is wanted in ... pretty much everywhere, lots of bounties. She sought refuge at Hollow Hold about nine cycles ago, been here ever since."

"And she knows where the Suth'ra are?" Zoey said to Dork.

"Aye," Dork said under a waning confidence.

"And you can take us to her?"

"Aye." Dork pointed to a small tunnel entrance about a hundred meters away. "She frequents an establishment just through that corridor."

Zoey's eyes followed the mangled footpath back to their landing platform, passing various dingy outlets along the way. Sleazy merchants guarded the entrances to their respective shops while shady locals manned the various alleyways. As she surveyed the shifty silhouettes, Zoey caught the faint reflections of numerous watching eyes. The occasional ember of tobacco outlined the stony face of its owner. Her eyes remained cold and focused on the task at hand, but her mind recoiled at the thought of proceeding.

"Lead the way," she said, nodding to Dork.

Dork returned her nod and about-faced. With a swing of his flabby arms, he began to waddle off the platform and towards the corridor entrance. Zoey walked close behind, followed by Max and Ross. Perra brought up the rear, scanning the vicinity with vigilant eyes. The clanks of heavy footsteps across the grated metal panes caught the attention of every creature within earshot. Reddened eyes and steely expressions followed their every move, peering through clouds of smoke expelled from lungs and machinery. Walking the winding path meant minding a delicate balance while ducking under steaming pipes and squeezing around narrow, railless corners. Hollow Hold radiated the kind of perilous environment that would give health and safety inspectors heart attacks on sight. A patchwork of function to say the least; more like a jumbled mishmash of nightmare-inducing scaffolding held together by strips of duct tape and slivers of hope.

Dork paused at the entrance of a long and narrow corridor about a hundred meters in length. Ropes of fiber optics dangled from the ceiling, lighting the passage with slits at random intervals. Gusts of dank air lifted thin clouds of soot that stung eyes and choked lungs. The width of the tunnel allowed for two standard humanoids to pass each other in relative comfort, although a beast the size of Dork made traversing a bit awkward. As the group assembled in front of the entrance, Zoey peered down the tunnel and noticed an array of colors dancing at the end.

"What is that?" she said.

"Market," Dork said.

"What kind of market?"

"Every kind."

With an abject sigh, Dork ducked his head and began his slow, lumbering plod down the tunnel. The group followed one-by-one with Perra acting as an anchor. She used a cautious sidestep to keep a watchful eye on the rear. The occasional ambler squeezed by Dork, only to pause and stare down the obvious newcomers. Perra maintained eye contact with each curious local until they lost interest and returned to their own shady business. An assortment of colors and sounds brightened as the group neared the exit. Drumming beats and bustling conversation echoed down the corridor, that all-too-familiar buzz of commerce.

Dork emerged from the tunnel and stepped aside, allowing each member of the group to absorb the onslaught of sight and sound as they entered the vast bazaar. Max's jaw fell open as his disbelieving eyes struggled to ingest the tidal wave of visuals. An open-air market teeming with activity spread out in every direction. Countless patrons of all races and sizes rumbled along the massive grated walkway. Max glanced to the left, then to the right, then left, then right again, unable to locate an end to the sea of bodies and merchants. An infinite variety of signs and booths filled the craggy walls, some hawking their wares in the open air, others nestled into shallow caves. Numerous food carts rolled through the thick crowds, belching a stew of funky aromas. Max lifted his astounded gaze to the grated ceiling a few meters above, uncovering yet another massive floor of perpetual commerce; then another, and another, on and on without end. While the shadows of feet clanked overhead, the tops of heads passed below in yet another endless expanse, floor after floor of multi-leveled vendors and patrons.

"This way," Dork said, motioning towards a cabled platform.

Ross nudged Max out of a stupefied stare, allowing the group to follow. The whines of stressed metal settled into a dull background roar as untold numbers of local residents trekked along the shoddy promenades. Max's jaw refused to rejoin his face as his saucer-like eyes drank in the biological diversity. Spotted tentacles dangled from furrowed faces, parched and brittle due to the dry air. Gaping mouths grew yellowed fangs that would make a saber-toothed tiger blush. The slitted eyes of reptilian humanoids came in several non-paired configurations. A plumpish insectoid with a purple belly reminded Max of his brief time as an eggplant. Never in his wildest dreams had he conceived of such a place.

The group stepped onto an unstable platform, each corner attached to a thick woven cable. A large operating lever rested in the center, with which Dork seemed familiar. He dropped a meaty hand upon the rusty handle and pulled backwards. The platform began to sink at a slow and steady pace while filling the immediate area with needling creaks. It wobbled and pitched as it fell deeper into the cavern. At the fifth floor down, Dork thrust the lever back to a neutral position, stopping the lift with an abrupt thump.

"This way, almost there," he said, leading the group off the platform.

"Where are we going?" Ross said.

"The Rusty Spigot. A popular place for her kind."

"Blackmailers?"

"No. Well, yes. Politicians."

"Nifan is a politician?" Perra said.

Dork chuckled. "Aye, but not in the sense you might be thinking. It is true that Hollow Hold is one of the purest anarchies in the universe. However, power here is not measured by things like strength or numbers. It is measured by information. Those who have it rule by the invisible fist of influence. Those who don't, are simply ruled."

Zoey glanced back at Perra, who returned a look of concern. Dork continued his bumbling stride towards a dingy alleyway, knocking shoulders with any unfortunate local that got in his way. His broad profile disappeared into the shadow of a jagged tunnel carved into the stone face between two shops. The sharp clanks of feet on metal softened as they transitioned onto solid rock. A dangling strip of pendant lights dropped fuzzy spots along the smooth walkway. Zoey peered over Dork's shoulder to find a hammered metal sign attached to the rear of the tunnel. A string of alien characters ended with the etched outline of a dripping spigot, confirming the location.

As the group rounded the corner, the gnashing sounds of commerce faded into the background, replaced by the calming ambience of a chic lounge. Immense columns of polished rock connected floor to ceiling. Elaborate inlays and colorful stonework glistened around the room. An eclectic arrangement of plush couches and lounge chairs filled the space, housing an equally eclectic arrangement of humanoid occupants. A small team of waiters in dainty uniforms glided around the den, serving drinks and refreshments to their esteemed clientele. The dull roars of conversation served as an audible backdrop. A thin haze of smoke snaked its way around the lounge as the collective exhales of relaxed regulars. All shapes, sizes, and colors of eyes turned towards Dork as the only visitor wearing tattered garments. The place radiated class as if unaware of its unclassy location. Despite the distinct awkwardness of Dork's presence, the jazz band in the corner played on as if nothing were amiss.

Dork stopped in the middle of the room and surveyed the space through squinting eyes, emitting the occasional grunt of concentration. The group cluttered behind him like a pod of wayward ducklings. Meddling eyes turned away to rejoin their conversations in progress. Zoey scrutinized the chamber with a leery gaze while Perra kept a watchful eye on the entrance. Ross turned his lazy-eyed indifference to Max, who had dropped a stupefied stare for one of childlike glee.

"Why are you so giddy?" Ross said.

"Do you know where we are?" Max said.

Ross glanced away for a moment and returned with one raised eyebrow. "A rocky hellhole of despair?"

"No." Max leaned in with a whisper. "We're in the *Star Wars* cantina. Just look around at all these crazy aliens. Hell, they even have the creepy band."

Ross raised the other eyebrow and took another look around. "Huh, I'll be damned."

"If they play that same tune over and over, I'll die a happy nerd."

Ross put an imaginary flute to his lips. "Do dit, do dit, do dit doooo ..."

Max delved into his best alien thug impression, then tapped Perra on the shoulder while gesturing to Ross. "He doesn't like you."

Ross snorted in amusement.

Perra responded with a confused look.

Max dropped a hand on her shoulder. "I don't like you either."

Ross and Max snickered like preteen boys reacting to a dick joke.

Zoey spun around with the glare of a perturbed mother. "Will you guys shut up?"

Perra rolled her eyes as Max and Ross bowed their heads like scolded children.

"There," Dork said, pointing to a dim corner of the lounge. "That's Nifan, in the green head wrap."

The group refocused their collective attention onto the quiet corner in question. Nifan, her face obscured by silky fabric, chatted with a nameless cohort inside a chesterfield booth. The red leather and rounded visage radiated a mafia vibe. She turned to capture the attention of a passing waiter, revealing her ashen skin and cobalt eyes. Perra consulted her comdev for a visual confirmation.

"That's her," Perra said.

"Good, let's go," Zoey said, jabbing Dork in the back.

"What?" Dork dropped into a harsh whisper and tossed a bulging eye over his shoulder. "No, you go. I'm done. I fulfilled my end of the deal."

"No you haven't," Zoey said, also in a harsh whisper. "I asked if you knew someone who knew the Suth'ra. You said yes. You said it was Nifan. We don't know if she knows and I'm not about to trust you on your word. Until we know, you stay."

"Do I look like someone who keeps company with politicians?"

"Do I look like someone who cares?"

"I have a reputation to consider."

"What reputation? You're a street con."

Dork paused for a moment, then grumbled. "Fine, let's just get this over with."

The group followed Dork's lumbering lead in a single file line, squeezing through a small maze of couches and disgruntled onlookers. Nifan tilted her head to acknowledge her blubbery visitor just before he arrived at the booth. Without so much as a kind glance, she waved her tablemate away with a limp gesture. The seedy humanoid departed with haste as Dork took his final steps. The group followed one by one, emerging from behind his bulky frame. Nifan eyed each new visitor as they crowded around the booth. Her angular brow and sharpened cheekbones sank into layers of shimmering green fabric. Pops of color erupted from several gaudy rings and an ornate necklace. Matted blue sashes offered an icy complement to haunting eyes, a detail Zoey understood as kempt and fashion-conscious. She knew right away that Nifan considered herself a socialite as much as a politician.

"Dork," Nifan said with a dose of disdain. "To what do I owe the pleasure of your ... company?"

"Madam Nifan," Dork said, trying and failing to sound proper. "I bring you informants."

"Informants?" Nifan raked a skeptical gaze over the group. "And what could these filthy drifters possibly offer me?"

"That depends on what you have to offer us," Zoey said.

Nifan hurled a visual dagger at Zoey. "Do not mistake your standing position for the higher ground. It would behoove you to know where you are and to whom you speak."

"You are a trafficker of information, are you not?"

"I prefer the term politician."

"I prefer the term blackmailing bitch."

Dork gasped as only a walrus could. Max, Ross, and Perra all turned stunned gazes to Zoey, now locked into a staring contest with Nifan. Without breaking eye contact, Zoey lowered her mask and hood, revealing deep orange skin, a scaly blue neck, and choppy black hair. Nifan raised her chin and puckered her smoky gray lips, sideswiped by an unexpected intrigue. Dispelling the tension, she sighed and swung an open palm across the table.

"Won't you and your companions have a seat?"

She sipped her steaming cup of tea, eyeing her guests as they settled around the milky marble table. Ross entered the circular booth first and shuffled around to Nifan's side, close enough to smell her pungent perfume, but far enough away to remain conscious. Max followed, then Perra. Zoey filled the aisle seat across from Nifan. Dork, without a viable seat, stood by himself and awaited instructions.

"Go wait by the bar," Nifan said without making eye contact.

"Yes, madam," Dork said, then bowed and waddled away.

Nifan watched over her shoulder as Dork tested the structural integrity of a barstool. "Silly creature," she said before returning her attention to Zoey. "So, how did you become entangled with it?"

"He tried to shake us down for credits. We turned the tables for information. He brought us here, to you."

"Does he know who you are?"

"No. I don't credit street cons with an overabundance of intelligence. Him even less so."

Nifan chuckled. "I would not discount your reputation here, especially within these walls. I dare say The Omen is the most distinguished guest the Spigot has ever seen."

"An empty compliment considering the clientele."

"Indeed." Nifan smirked, then eyed the group one by one. "So who are your companions?"

Zoey turned to the masked faces sitting beside her. Starting with Perra, she pointed her way down the line. "This one is Not, that one is Your, and the last one is Business. He's a feisty one."

Ross winked.

Nifan grinned as she studied Zoey's face. "Fair enough. Speaking of business, it seems we may have some to discuss. You are looking for information. What kind?"

"We are looking for the identities and whereabouts of specific residents."

"Hmm, must be higher profiles if you are sitting here. Who?"

"The disgraced members of the Suth'ra."

Nifan leaned back in the booth, her ashy face taut with a toothy grin. "Unfortunately for you, *that* is some expensive information."

"Only if you actually have it."

"Oh yes, I have it. There are three of them. All three live in the perilous lower core. One is insane, in the purest sense of the word. One is guarded and nomadic, call him retired. The third continues his research inside a hidden laboratory."

"Where?"

"Silly girl, that's the expensive part. What do you offer in payment?"

"What do you want?" Zoey struggled to maintain her poker face.

Nifan extended an arm draped in silky green cloth and tapped a fingertip on the table. "In this place, if you do not know what you have to offer, then you have nothing to offer."

Max's puzzled eyes followed the verbal tennis match, now resting in Zoey's court. Perra's hands fidgeted atop her lap as she scanned the room for advantageous positions. Ross decided to kill time by testing the booth's scratch resistance, of which it had none. Zoey and Nifan stared into each other's hardened eyes in cold silence. Their motionless bodies mirrored each other, facing off like coiled cobras ready to strike. Sensing weakness, Nifan allowed a sly smirk to creep across her face. She leaned forward and folded her hands on the table. Her confident glare bathed Zoey in intellectual dominance, forcing beads of sweat to leak from her brow. With a subtle nod, Nifan summoned a rakish suit stretched around a pillar of muscle. Lifting itself from a wall, it began trudging towards the table. Zoey slipped a hand under her cloak and around the handle of her plasma gun.

"Okay then," Ross said. "Let's wrap this up, kitty needs to piss."

Ross leaned over and whispered into Nifan's ear. Her piercing gaze melted from her skull, leaving her face limp and lifeless. A shaking hand lifted to cover her slacking jaw as watering eyes lowered to the table. Cloudy tears streamed down her cheek and onto her fingers. She filled her lungs with floundering gasps, trying to maintain her composure. Rising from the booth, she turned away and dropped her face into both hands. Her body heaved with grief, but the environment and her reputation prevented an outburst of emotion. She waved off the approaching bodyguard and paused to digest the reveal. Steady and weighted breaths helped to regain a sliver of self-control. Turning back to the group, she offered a slow nod to the floor before lifting a humbled gaze to Zoey.

"His name is Hagramead Limpara, formerly known in the Suth'ra Society as Halim. His laboratory is located in the fourth tier of the lower core, section 82, service tunnel six. Look for a tarnished steel door with black rivets. Knock twice, wait, then knock twice again. Tell him that the Spigot flows." Nifan turned and smiled at Ross. "Thank you."

"No worries," Ross said, then turned a nonchalant gaze to the gawking eyes of his stunned companions. "Shall we?"

Nifan returned to her seat and bowed her head while the rest of the group shuffled out the other side. Her deflated gaze fell upon the cup of tea resting on the table, now cold from neglect. A wayward finger traced the rim as her troubled mind fought for abatement. The cup rattled in its plate as Dork plopped himself at the other side of the booth, knocking Nifan out of thought. The wave of impact jostled everything in a short radius, including Nifan, provoking a huff and eye roll. Turning away from her bumbling minion, she caught a glimpse of the sling pack over Zoey's shoulder as the group disappeared down the entrance corridor.

"Are you well, madam?" Dork said.

Nifan responded with a conniving gaze. "Send word to Lord Essien. Inform her that her prize is en route to Halim."

CHAPTER 15

Zoey and her band of masked hoodlums clanked onto the rickety lift. She grasped the control lever and thrust it forward, causing the platform to jostle about before climbing the rusty cables. As the conveyer whined with ascent, she turned a suspicious gaze to Ross, who seemed immune to the obvious tension.

"What did you say to Nifan?" Zoey said.

"I told her what she needed to know," Ross said.

"Which was?"

He batted an eye at Zoey. "What she needed to know."

"Care to share?" Perra said.

"Not really."

"You don't have to be a dick about it," Max said.

"Not being a dick. Just respecting Kenny's wishes."

"And what were those?"

Ross sighed and tossed a brief glare to Max. "Don't give away anything you don't have to."

Max sneered as if debating a brick wall.

Ross glanced around at nothing in particular. "Oh, and by the way, you're all welcome for saving your arses back there, *again*. Don't thank me all at once."

Zoey yanked the lever back, stopping the lift at their original floor. Without a word, she tromped off the teetering platform and pushed towards the passage leading back to the ship. Max followed with a combination of speed walking and stutter jogging. Ross swished around pedestrians with the grace of a swashbuckling pirate. Perra, nose-deep in her comdev, brought up the rear. Her inattention required several apologies as she bumped shoulders with random vagrants.

Their collective footsteps softened as they entered the rocky tunnel. Zoey soldiered down the corridor with a focused stride, shunning the glares of passing locals. Perra stopped about halfway through, her slack-jawed expression illuminated by the comdev in her hands.

"Hold up, something's wrong," Ross said.

The group halted and backtracked to Perra, who stood stunned and motionless.

"What's the problem?" Zoey said.

Perra lifted a distressed face. "She did say *Halim*, right? H-a-l-i-m?"

"Yes. Why?"

"I thought that name sounded vaguely familiar. You and I had only heard stories growing up, but no one ever mentioned his ties to the Suth'ra. Halim, the Warlord of Draco, the military genius responsible for most of the universe's advanced weaponry. That was his field of study. That's why he was kicked out. Even the Suth'ra saw him as too dangerous for the greater good. *That* is who we are going to see."

Zoey stood speechless in a rare moment of trepidation.

"A military genius?" Max said. "What, like a Sun Tzu or something?"

"Hardly," Ross said. "This certifiable psycho makes Sun Tzu look like an ornery kid with a pellet gun. Halim is responsible, and I mean personally responsible, for some of the most brutal and bloody intergalactic wars the 'verse has ever seen. Wars that have resulted in more deaths than all of human history combined, millions of times over. This one guy has snuffed out entire civilizations with the apathy of extinguishing a cigarette."

"Legend has it," Perra said, "he once worked for the enormous Xerocan Empire that controlled a full quarter of the supercluster. Under the fog of war, he leaked secrets among the empire's four main rivals, ensuring their mutual destructions. Trillions and trillions of innocent beings, poof, gone, all for the advancement of military strategy. Some say he was tortured and executed, others say he escaped and lives in exile, the latter being the apparent reality."

"Nifan has to know that, right?" Max said.

"Yes," Zoey said, staring at the tunnel wall. "That is a massive piece of leverage, one she would never give away lightly." She turned a bewildered gaze to Ross. "So why give it to us?"

"That," Ross said, pointing at Zoey, "is a damn good question."

* * *

The bustling control bridge of Lord Essien's battlecruiser halted with an abrupt silence. All eyes lifted to Essien, her arms spread across the railing of the observation deck. Using every ounce of composure to maintain said composure, she eyed the giant hologram of Dork with the bitter contempt of a wife discovering that her husband had boinked her best friend. The rigid leather of her black uniform popped across her chest as muscles tightened all over her body. Her hands paled as she squeezed the blood from her veins.

"Excuse me?" she said with a graveled voice.

Dork gulped. "Nifan says—"

"I heard you the first time you paunchy piece of shit. Put Nifan on. Right. Now."

Dork glanced off to his side, then nodded. His glowing image crumbled into a dance of static and reformed into the silky bust of Nifan.

"Lord Essien," Nifan said with a sigh of indifference. "What a unique ... pleasure."

Essien narrowed her eyes. "Don't you dare talk down to me after sending your dumpy lapdog to drop that bomb. You mean to tell me that Halim, *the* Halim, resides in that sewer of a planet?" She paused for effect, then waved an arm in dismissal. "Nevermind, don't answer, I don't care. What I *really* want to know is actually quite simple. Tell me, why oh why, did you send bitch Bryx to that madman ... with MY PROPERTY?! We had a deal!"

Nifan chuckled. "Silly girl, you know what happens when better deals come along."

Essien's face twisted with the flames of unbridled rage. Shadowy slits of taut skin spidered across her whitewashed complexion. Black lips receded around gnashing teeth as her silver irises pulsed under twitching eyelids. "You do know what this means."

"Yes ... I do." Nifan smirked before her image crumbled into nothing.

Essien heaved with anger and slammed her fists on the railing over and over. "Fuck! Fuck! Fuck! Fuck! Fuuuuuck!" She turned to the hard-nosed lieutenant standing beside her and punched him in the face, unleashing a tidal wave of fury that sent the poor fool tumbling over the railing and onto the control room floor. The heavy impact of armor on metal echoed around the room, producing an array of terrified faces. All eyes remained fixated on Essien as she stomped around the observation deck. "Summon all warships to our location! Prep the Rippers! Get them all here, now! If it's war that backstabbing bitch wants, then it's war I will bring her!" She whipped a rigid arm to the com controller, who flinched at the force of her assertion. "You! Get Jai on the com!"

* * *

A fresh bead of drool fell from the corner of Jai Ferenhal's meaty jaw, adding to a small puddle on his pilot suit. Wet, rumbling snores bellowed from his open throat, causing cheeks to flutter with every exhale. Hollow Hold's rusty horizon filled the viewport, but his shuttered eyes resigned themselves to a complete lack of interest. A limp hand lost its grip on the control yoke, causing the Ripper to list with a slow tilt. The neighboring pilot sneered at the intrusion before thrusting out of harm's way. The fleet of a dozen ships reassembled, having failed to locate their target. They floated above the horizon in a triangular formation, waiting for their commander to resume consciousness.

The crackling static of an incoming transmission knocked Jai out of his unwarranted nap. A few headshakes and lip smacks restored a menacing persona. The hologram image of a livid Lord Essien appeared above the console.

"Lord Ess—"

"Shut up, you incompetent twat!" Lord Essien said with a shower of saliva that the transmission technology deemed worthy of visualizing.

Jai's lips retreated into his mouth.

"Do you have any idea of how horribly you have failed me? Any at all?"

Jai's broadened eyes darted back and forth inside his sweating skull. "Uh—"

"Bryx slipped through. She's inside, and as you sit there looking like an addlebrained idiot, she and the others are delivering the package to Halim."

Jai's brow collapsed. "Halim? *The* Halim?"

Essien rolled her eyes. "No, Halim the Hollow Hold gardener."

"But I thought—"

"Don't, you'll hurt yourself." Essien sighed and shook her head before returning a vengeful gaze. "Listen. It's very simple. Bryx is there. She is taking the package to Halim. Yes, *the* Halim, somewhere inside that rock. I am assembling the armada and will bring all-out fucking war upon that planet in less than 30 parks. In the meantime, your job, your only job, is to FIND FUCKING BRYX!"

"I shall not fail you Lor—"

"Stop talking, you overgrown frog turd! Go! Go! Go!"

Essien's infuriated image crumbled from view, allowing Jai's lungs to deflate. A few slaps to the face and a shift in posture mended his focus. He established a comlink to the Ripper fleet, piecing together a hologram grid of Varokin faces.

"Bryx got through. She and the others are inside. Put marks on all MX class freighters under level four. Pick your targets, investigate, keep me informed. Lord Essien's entire fleet will be in orbit in less than 30 parks. We have until then to acquire the package."

"But sir," a random minion said. "The local powers will not take kindly to Varokin Rippers entering the cave system. Lord Essien still has many enemies here."

"I know." Jai sighed and raked a somber gaze over the derelict planet. He gnawed his lips, then lifted a hardened chin to the minion grid. "Prepare for war. Break formation. All weapons loose."

The fleet acquired their targets, broke ranks, and sped towards the surface.

* * *

Zoey emerged from the musky corridor, followed by Ross, Max, and Perra. Beams of sunlight reflected off the tangled web of pipes and scaffolding, trapping motes of dust inside their wakes. The sharp clanks of rubber soles atop suspended metal sheets acquired a crop of onlookers once again. The group shunned the attention as best they could, opting for resolute strides as they tromped down a maze of shoddy walkways. Rounding a steaming pipe, Zoey caught the silhouette of her tiny freighter hiding behind a thin wall of haze, still resting atop the rickety landing pad. The leery eyes of locals followed their every move while adding puffs of lung smoke to the choking smog. Without incident, the group set foot onto the landing pad, allowing each to breathe a sigh of relief. As Perra stepped onto the platform, her comdev erupted with warning chirps.

"What is it?" Zoey said, stopping cold and turning to Perra.

Max, still disoriented by the rancid smell, walked into the back of Ross.

Perra fished the comdev from her pocket and checked the alert. "Shit! Ripper inbound! Move!"

The group sprinted towards the freighter about 20 meters away.

Before they reached the airlock, a Ripper ship fell into a hover above the parked vessel, its tentacled arsenal spread and ready for attack. Zoey threw her arms out wide, stopping the group's advance. The Ripper's fiery thrusters shook the landing pad and stirred up choking clouds of dust. They squinted as the rushing exhaust assaulted their bodies and fluttered their cloaks. Several locals disappeared into shops and alleys while others looked on with mild curiosity.

"Zoey Bryx," the minion said in a hissing voice through an external speaker. "Stand down and hold your position. Everyone place your hands upon your heads."

Zoey paused for a moment, then turned to the group and nodded. They all complied.

"Now remove the package and place it at your feet."

After a hefty sigh and grimace, she swung the strap over her shoulder and lowered the pack to the ground.

The minion grinned and switched to fleet com. "Target acquired, Master Jai. Lock onto my position. I shall hold them here until y—"

Without warning, a missile shrieked up from the cavern depths and slammed into the Ripper, destroying the ship in a massive ball of fire. The blast wave knocked all four onto their backs and cracked the landing pad. Shrapnel rained in all directions, snapping pipes, shattering glass, and crippling walkways.

"Take cover!" Zoey said, scooping up the sling pack.

The group scrambled to their feet and stumbled towards the ship, trying to maintain their balance on the swaying platform. They dove underneath the frame and hid behind the landing gear as slivers of red hot metal bounced off the hull. Clanks of falling debris faded into the distance, leaving the crackling flames of burning remnants. Despite the utter shock, Max welcomed the contrasting aroma of flaming fuel and sulfur.

"Well that was unexpected," Ross said with his usual flat affect.

"What the hell just happened?" Max said.

"I have no idea," Perra said, eyeing the smoldering air the Ripper had occupied. Her comdev erupted with another series of warning chirps.

"Let's go," Zoey said.

She skittered out from beneath the ship, opened the airlock, and ushered the group inside. Lifting her gaze to the cavern entrance far above, she spotted a group of spidery ships racing towards them. With a burst of adrenaline, she leapt into the ship and slapped the interior wall panel, sealing the airlock behind her. Perra, already strapped into the co-pilot chair, danced her arms across the control panel, igniting engines and prepping for departure. Zoey raced into the cockpit and threw herself into the pilot's chair.

"Status?" she said, strapping herself down.

"Thrusters online," Perra said. "Launch prep complete, main engines spinning up." She tapped her way down a row of red icons. "Weapons online."

"Gravy," Zoey said and slapped a palm on the thruster control. A dull roar engulfed the cabin as tight blue flames spilled from the undercarriage. She pulled back on the yoke, lifting the ship from the platform. The landing gear retracted as the freighter floated out into the cave interior. Flashing red lights and warning sirens filled the cockpit as Ripper ships locked on to their position from above. Max and Ross strapped themselves into the wall seats behind Zoey and Perra. "Hang on to something," Zoey said, then pitched the ship downward into the massive cave. Perra pointed and screamed as she spotted four missiles tearing towards them out of the blackness. Max followed her lead and indulged in a high-pitched scream of his own. Ross cocked his ears back and glared at Max while Zoey ignited lead thrusters, hoping to outmaneuver the attack. She rolled the ship to the side, but the missiles did not follow. They screamed by, rumbling the hull as they sped towards their intended targets. A series of deafening explosions rocked the cavern as the missiles obliterated several Ripper ships, raining fire and metal into the cave. Zoey and Perra traded bewildered glances. The main engines pinged green. Zoey thrust the yoke forward and raced down into the rocky depths.

"Bring up the nav grid," Zoey said.

Perra complied.

The viewport projected a geometric representation of the cave system, allowing Zoey to pilot in the darkness.

"Three Rippers still on our tail," Perra said, consulting the beacon scanner.

"Gonna try to lose 'em," Zoey said.

She yanked the yoke to the side and ignited the bow thrusters, steering the vessel around a sharp corner. All three Rippers followed, matching Zoey's every move. A white-hot incinerator beam shot past the ship, prompting Zoey to thrust upwards into a narrow cave while shouting an array of curses. Floodlights streaked past the viewport, painting the tunnel in thin strips of light. A dangling pipe scraped the vessel, sending shrieks throughout the cabin. The targeting siren erupted, followed by the pings of an incoming missile. Zoey ignited all landing thrusters and dropped the yoke to a lower corner. The ship carved the wall, spitting sparks as it drifted around a hairpin turn and into another tunnel. The missile screeched by and detonated in the open air, sending shockwaves through the caves. Two of the Rippers managed to follow, but the last slammed into the junction corner and exploded on impact.

"One down," Zoey said.

"Fantastic," Perra said, then turned to the rear. "How are you guys doing back there?"

Max responded with a horrified face that one might use for a crippling bout of diarrhea.

Ross lifted his head from grooming his forearm. "What?"

Another series of warning sirens filled the cockpit. Red lights flashed all around, followed by the pings of several incoming missiles.

"There!" Perra pointed to a massive cave intersection ahead with an open central hub that resembled a hollow sea urchin. "Can you make it?"

"No choice," Zoey said. "Divert anything you can to give us a boost."

Perra rerouted auxiliaries, giving the engines a surge of power. As the ship neared the enormous junction, a green pane of energy formed around the tunnel exit.

"What the hell is that?!" Perra said.

"Don't know." Zoey blasted it with ion cannons. The barrier absorbed the beams, reducing them to brief pulses of dissipated energy. "Shit!" Her eyes darted between the missile pings and the green barrier, unsure of what to do. "We have to try and punch through. Hold on!"

The entire group, minus Ross, screamed as the ship slammed into the barrier, but the freighter passed through without a scratch. The speeding missiles hit the barrier and disintegrated on impact, spraying puffs of metallic dust into the open core. The Rippers continued their pursuit, but met the exact same demise. They shattered into dust clouds, showering their remnants as a brilliant speckled mist. The targeting sirens ceased, leaving the cabin to heavy panting and the lapping of Ross's tongue.

Zoey spun the ship around to survey the aftermath, but found only the sparkles of cinders as they fell into the darkness below. The ship settled into a hover inside the massive cavern. A myriad of cave entrances decorated the rocky walls, outlined by rusty piping and dim floodlights. Support cables and steel beams attached themselves to the rock, but reeked of neglect and disrepair. A handful of patchwork walkways wound around the interior, serving as little more than rickety overlooks. The group stared at the green energy barrier that had saved their hides before it broke with static and faded away.

"What was that thing?" Perra said.

"I have no idea," Zoey said. "But whatever it was, it liked us more than them."

"A security feature, maybe?"

"Seems like a good guess. Let's hope they continue to favor us."

Perra turned to Max. "You okay?"

Max closed his eyes, took a deep breath, and nodded his head. "Nope."

Perra grinned and turned to Ross. "How about you?"

"Right as rain. Still could use that piss though." Ross unbuckled himself from the seat and disappeared down the cockpit corridor.

"So where are we?" Zoey said, her gaze still affixed to the cave exit.

"Let's see." Perra swiped the control panel, lifting a hologram map of the cave complex. She tapped the pulsing beacon that signaled their location. The grid zoomed to the coordinates, showing a webbed network of tiers and tunnels. After a brief study, she let out a conclusive grunt. "Looks like we are on the sixth tier of the lower core. Where did Nifan say again?"

"Fourth tier, section 82."

"Okay." Perra expanded the grid with both hands and pointed to a nearby branch. "That would be here." She tapped the area and applied the coordinates to the nav grid, setting a new destination. Lifting from the co-pilot chair, she stretched her neck and gazed out the viewport. She scanned the lower rock face while biting her cheek, then pointed to the entrance of a large service tunnel. "That's the one. That's where we need to go."

"Good work," Zoey said and offered a high five.

Perra slapped it with a toothy smile before returning to her seat.

The hull thrusters rumbled underfoot as Zoey reoriented the ship towards the tunnel. She ignited the main engines and kicked the vessel forward, resulting in a loud thump from the cargo bay.

"Bloody hell!" Ross said from distance. "Warn a kitty next time!"

CHAPTER 16

A thick cloud of black smoke poured over the rim of the massive cave entrance, like a witch cauldron boiling on the planet surface. It churned as the billowing remnants of the Varokin Ripper fleet, adding its own choking flare to the collective pollution. While swirling and minding its own smoggy business, Jai's Ripper ship punched through the top, followed by a screeching missile in hot pursuit. From a distance, the scene offered an amusing perspective, like a silvery snake chasing a black squid after a failed ink fart diversion.

Inside the cockpit, Jai abandoned his usual threatening persona for one of complete and utter terror. Sweat poured from his forehead and into his bulging eyes. The salty stings of pain had no effect on his concentration, a laser-like focus dedicated to non-death. His grumbling voice had morphed into the high-pitched squeals of a frightened schoolgirl, sucking any and all menace right out of the cabin.

The red flashes and blaring sirens of his imminent demise filled the cockpit. The ship raced towards orbit with engines ablaze, but with nowhere to run or hide, the bitter end closed around him. Fate, always clever despite its nonexistence, decided to throw him a bone. Jai buzzed a small satellite in his blinding effort to not die, spinning it into his wake. The missile slammed into the unfortunate satellite,

ZACHRY WHEELER

blowing it to smithereens and pissing off every resident with a holo-gram projector.

Jai released the yoke and floated in the safety of orbit, panting and sweating with the stunned expression of a foogog having sur-vived a flogging gauntlet (or some other reasonable comparison). He removed his helmet, tossed it aside, and wiped his forehead with the sleeve of his pilot suit. His eyelids returned from a jaunt behind his eyeballs, allowing him to indulge in a few darkened moments of adrenaline flushing. After a string of fluttering breaths, he opened his eyes to the blackness of space. Or rather, to the sudden appearance of Lord Essien's towering cruiser as it blinked out of hyperspace.

Jai's toddler-like squeal returned as he rolled the Ripper to avoid a collision. The immediate rush of additional adrenaline exited his body with several stiff punches to the control panel. The console, unaware of what it had done to deserve such hostility, responded in anger with shrill error pings. Knowing that Lord Essien would hail him at any moment, Jai established a hasty comlink with his Ripper fleet. None responded, prompting a vigorous facepalm. At that mo-ment, of course, the hologram bust of Lord Essien pieced itself to-gether above the control panel. Jai slid his meaty palm down his face and plunked it onto the armrest with the resigned acceptance of a corrupt auditee.

"Lor—" Jai said.

"Do you have the package?" Lord Essien said, in no mood for pleasantries.

"No."

"Where is the rest of the fleet?"

"Destroyed."

"And why are you still breathing?"

"I escaped. Barely."

Lord Essien closed her eyes and shook her head before donning a disappointed grimace. "You know, I'd like to be surprised, but I'm really not." Her casual demeanor caught Jai off guard. "Remind me, why do I keep you alive?"

Jai thought for a moment. "Entertainment?"

Essien snorted.

Jai ruffled his brow, unsure of whether she conveyed amusement, disgust, or both.

"Dock with the cruiser and meet me on the bridge. As much as it pains me to say it, I may still need you. Someone has to clean the shitters in this place."

"Yes, Lord Ess—"

The hologram image crumbled into nothing before Jai could complete his grovel. As he sulked inside a one-man pity party, an enormous armada of battlecruisers, Rippers, and assault ships blinked out of hyperspace.

* * *

Zoey engaged the landing thrusters and lowered the ship onto the jagged ground in front of service tunnel six, or rather, what Perra had counted and concluded as service tunnel six. The cave system narrowed when approaching the core, necessitating the use of smaller and smaller vessels. The main corridor into section 82 of lower-tier four proved almost impassable, even for the tiny freighter. The curved walls of craggy rock made landing a wee bit stressful. But Zoey, always a calm and capable pilot, managed to settle the craft without tearing a hole in the hull. The three landing claws gripped the uneven surface at an awkward but secure angle. Other pilots had not been so lucky and the evidence of their incompetence decorated the cavern floors.

The lower core was a mine in every sense of the word. At peak production, it hummed with the perpetual activity of professional miners, both humanoid and robot. Tunnels in the core remained small in scope in order to maintain the structural integrity of the planet they pierced. A hollowed-out core meant that gravity could claim its prize, resulting in a much smaller planet and a lot of dead miners. Therefore, engineers went to great lengths to ensure the rigidity of the lower core. As a result, tunnels stayed small and miners mined the old-fashioned way: with hover packs and laser picks. Robots worked as mules, using conveyors and hover carts to transport ore to service shuttles.

Most service tunnels were the height and width of a single humanoid, two at most. Their primary purpose was to 1) connect adjacent corridors, hence the service, and 2) store mining tools inside numerous small rooms carved along their interiors. Once the miners abandoned the planet, these service tunnel rooms became ideal hideaways for anyone needing to disappear. As time went on, the lower core became home to some of the most dangerous beings in the supercluster. Any who ventured into the lower core risked their lives at a baseline, hence the unwritten rule: know your knock, because it may be your last.

The airlock slid open, revealing Zoey and Perra with armed plasma pistols in hand. Due to the sultry conditions, the group had shed their cloaks in favor of mobility and comfort. Dim sconces along the cavern walls served as the primary lighting source, casting fuzzy rings around the dark brown rock. Zoey powered up a handheld spotlight and stepped onto the rocky surface first. The sling pack swayed on her shoulder as she pointed her gun and light down each side of the corridor. Max and Ross followed, dropping down to the tunnel floor with heavy thumps that kicked up small clouds of fine dust. Perra stepped down with a second spotlight and closed the airlock behind her.

Max coughed as tiny particles teased his lungs. "Ugh, it's so damn muggy down here. Smells like crotch."

"What did you expect?" Zoey said, annoyed that she needed to speak at all.

"I don't know, feels fine to me," Ross said.

"That's because cats are desert creatures," Max said, followed by another cough. "You'd feel at home in a Finnish sauna."

Ross raised an eyebrow. "Why Finnish?"

"Because Finland is cold and they like saunas."

"But saunas are hot no matter where they are. Finnish is an unnecessary qualifier."

"Will you guys shut up?" Zoey said, elevating her annoyance level.

"Just saying," Ross said. "It could be a Jamaican sauna, wouldn't change the heat."

"But, your perception of the heat *would* change," Max said. "What if the external temperature was hotter than the sauna?"

"Then why would you have a sauna?"

Zoey fired her plasma pistol into the opposite wall, rumbling the tunnel with a flash of static that showered pea-sized rocks over the group. Max and Ross froze in place and stared at her through widened eyes. Zoey glared at them as a thin cloud of dust enveloped the group. Ross sighed and shook the dust from his body, like a wet dog out of the rain. Max, still somewhat petrified, responded with a salute of respect. Perra rolled her eyes as Zoey turned for the service tunnel entrance. She paused at the mouth and shined her spotlight down into the depths, uncovering little more than rock and darkness.

"Steel door, black rivets," Perra said.

"Yup," Zoey said, then sighed with resignation. "Okay, let's get on with it."

She adjusted the sling pack and took the first few steps into the service tunnel with an outstretched plasma pistol. The group followed with Perra securing the rear as always. They passed the first door about 20 meters in, a plane of solid steel embedded into the rock. An eerie scrape caused Zoey to throw a fist into the air, signaling a stop. The group paused and stared at the door with quiet apprehension, but no sounds followed. Zoey dropped her hand and proceeded down the tunnel. They passed another door after 20 meters, then another, and another, studying each under the spotlight. The fifth door featured the telltale black rivets in a large X pattern across the face. Zoey turned and motioned for the group to stop. She gave a hand signal to Perra, who nodded and readied her weapon. Max and Ross stood motionless with their backs against the tunnel wall. Zoey raised a fist, took a deep breath, then knocked twice. *Thunk, thunk.* She waited a few ticks, then knocked twice again. *Thunk, thunk.* The door cracked open with a sudden clunk and whine, bathing the tunnel in a bright white light. Zoey skittered backwards with her weapon raised to the door. They waited for an immediate response; a greeting, an attack, but nothing came.

"Come in, come in," said a peppy voice from well inside the room.

Zoey glanced at shrugging Perra, then back to the door. "The Spig—"

"The Spigot flows, yes, yes, come in already."

Zoey tightened her grip on the plasma gun, pulled the door open, then stepped inside with a slow and cautious stride. Her jaw fell open as she scanned the pristine white room, the kind of room one would expect to see bunny suits assembling delicate computer chips. The ceiling loomed as a giant grid of diffused light, matching the floor in scope and scale. An enormous network of touch panels decorated the walls, their smooth black faces housing an ocean of blinking lights. The entire enclosure spanned the length of a football field with tables upon tables of assorted gadgets in various stages of assembly. The conditioned air offered a cool and welcome reprieve as they stepped inside.

"Close the door then," the voice said. "You're letting all the good air out."

Perra closed the door behind her, then recoiled as it locked and reset itself. Zoey struggled to find a bearing on the mystery voice. After a slow scan of the massive room, her squinting eyes fell upon a wee fellow with white hair and a white coat, standing about a meter high and facing the wall. His tiny hands darted around control panels, sending blips and chirps into the sterile air.

"Are you Halim?" Zoey said.

"In the flesh," Halim said, sounding like an overly caffeinated Irishman. "I take it you have brought me the shift drive core?"

"Wh—what?" Zoey narrowed her eyes. "How do you know that?"

"It's my job to know. Plus, Nifan told me all about it. She does love to play her games. Strange lass, that one. Lord Essien made a deal with her in order to find you, which set this whole plan into motion."

"Plan?"

"She did not tell you?"

Halim paused his furious hands and turned from the wall to address Zoey. His eyes almost jumped from their sockets when he saw her. He yelped like a frightened puppy and sought refuge behind the nearest table. Zoey caught a brief glimpse of his pale blue skin, bushy white beard, and matching eyebrows before he disappeared.

"What just happened?" she said, turning to the group.

Perra and Max shrugged while Ross groomed his bicep.

Zoey walked over to the table and peeked around the corner. Halim sat with his back to a table leg, panting and knocking his knuckles. They met eyes again. His terrified expression terrified itself even more, prompting a louder yelp before darting behind the next table. Zoey turned to the group and spread her arms in the universal WTF pattern. Out of nowhere, Max started laughing. Perra shrugged as Zoey slapped her arms to her side and glared at him. While wiping away tears, Max motioned for Zoey to return to the group. His belly laugh slowed to a snicker as she rejoined them.

"What's so funny?" she said in a harsh whisper.

"Don't you see?" Max said. "This is a former member of the Suth'ra. He's a giant nerd and you're smoking hot. He has no idea how to talk to you."

Zoey huffed. "You can't be serious."

Perra tilted her head. "He's afraid of us?"

"Yes. Well, kind of, in a manner of speaking. Listen, it's all about the wheelhouse. You know machines. Zoey knows trafficking. I know nerds. You're in my territory now, so let me work my magic."

Perra nodded.

Zoey sighed, rolled her eyes, then nodded.

"Okay, here's what I need you to do ..."

Max fell into a soft whisper as he relayed instructions to the Mulgawats. Halim's frightened eyes peered over a table, then disappeared with another yelp once Zoey caught them. Max concluded his spiel with a thumbs-up.

"Got it?"

"Again, you can't be serious," Zoey said.

"Trust me."

"I trust you," Perra said, then nodded at Zoey.

"Fine," Zoey said. "Do your thing."

A sharp clank on the floor caught everyone's attention. They turned to find Ross sitting on a table, shoving random items to the floor in order to gauge everyone's reaction.

"Bad kitty, stop that!" Max said.

Ross cocked his ears and reached for another item.

Max glared at him and turned back to Zoey. "Okay, give me the shift drive core."

She retrieved the device from her sling pack and handed it to Max.

"You two stay here. Watch for my signal."

Zoey unzipped her pilot suit, enough to show some respectable cleavage. "I hope you know what you're doing."

Max walked over to the table and plunked the shift drive core on top, rattling a crop of components and startling Halim into faint yip. "This is it, Rumac's amazing creation. It's a work of art, really." Max stared at the shiny ball with the admiration of a fanboy.

Halim peeked over the table with a skeptical gaze, his terrified expression morphing into contempt. Snatching a nearby stepping stool, he huffed and stomped himself to eye level. "*Art?* You call this blunder *art?* Rumac is a hack, a sniveling dabbler." Halim touched a fingertip to the drive core. "This was a lucky accident. Nothing more."

"If you say so," Max said with a cocky tone. "He did verify the multiverse."

Halim twitched his bushy eyebrows. "So? Any member of the Suth'ra could have done that given the desire. What was Rumac's field of study? Hyperspace? All he did was muse on space travel and develop jump cores. Pish posh, a halfwit child could construct better theories." Halim waved his hand in dismissal. "I, Halim, have elevated the art of war, a *true* art, to countless new paradigms. At this very instant, I am preparing to test a holistic planetary defense system, the first of its kind in the history of the universe." He balled his tiny fist and pumped it with the confidence one would expect from a narcissistic lunatic.

Max lowered a hand to his side and gave a subtle gesture to Zoey and Perra. The Mulgawats responded by giggling and twisting like infatuated fans. Zoey folded her hands at her waist and stiffened her arms, accentuating her already impressive bust. Perra bent one knee across the other and waved at Halim while batting her deep purple eyes. His overconfident persona descended into terror once again.

"Don't mind them," Max said. "They're just groupies, been following me around for months now." He winked at a dumbfounded Halim.

"*You?* Get to hit *that?*" Halim's jaw slacked.

Max up-nodded like an arrogant prick. "Mmhmm."

"Wow. What do you do?"

"I'm a max-level paladin. Earth class, retro build. I know the RPG servers inside and out." Max raised an open palm as if holding a crystal ball. "I can bend them to my every will like a cybernetic god. I'm a meme master, an arcane ninja."

Halim stroked his bushy beard. "Impressive."

"Well, not as impressive as this shiny little beauty." Max slapped a hand upon the shift drive core and narrowed his eyelids. "Which is why it needs to go. Like you said, hacks don't deserve such notoriety."

Halim nodded in nerd solidarity. "I completely agree."

"So what do you think? Can we take this sucker apart? I'm itching to see what's inside."

"Me too. In fact, I need one of its components to complete my own work, which is why Nifan sent you here. Lord Essien and her fleet should be in orbit by now. She and Nifan are on the brink of war, one that has been building for a very long time. However, it is Nifan who has the upper hand. Lord Essien will be the rather unfortunate test subject of my planetary defense system." Halim snorted with glee. "You actually got a taste of it on your way down here."

"Whoa, hold up, that was *your* work?" Max redirected his fanboy praise onto Halim. "Seriously, I have to say, I almost pissed myself when your missiles tore through those Rippers. And that energy net?" Max kissed his fingertips and exploded his palm like a proud Italian. "Beautiful work. Up high, my friend." Max offered a high five.

Halim leaned forward and completed the slap, albeit in a weak and clumsy manner.

Ross knocked another item to the floor and stared at Max.

"So anyway," Max said, ignoring the furry distraction. "Let's bust this hack ball open." He gave Zoey and Perra another subtle signal.

They responded with giggles, winks, and lower lip bites.

Max lowered his voice and leaned over the table. "Tell you what, if we can get this done quickly ..." He whispered a bon mot into Halim's ear.

Halim leaned back with a taut grin and nodded with the enthusiasm of a virgin at a brothel. His tiny hands nabbed the shift drive core and rolled it to his side of the table. After a few moments of careful study, he fished a tool from his pocket and started poking and prodding the surface. Panel after panel fell away, revealing a jumbled mess of wires, circuits, and delicate machinery. He detached piece after piece with the frantic hands of an orchestra conductor. Prudent eyes studied each part for usefulness before tossing it over his shoulder. A shower of components bounced off tables and clanked onto the floor. Ross batted at any flying object that sailed past him. Max raised a hand to cover his mouth, trying to mask the complete surprise that his plan worked. An exploded pile of remnants filled the table before Halim found his reward.

"Aha!" He lifted a tiny cylinder of pewter-like metal, about the size of a pen cap. "*This* is my prize."

Max rubbed his chin, trying to feign interest. "Hmm, interesting. Looks like, um ..." *Something smart-sounding.* "Expended ... neutronian ... kryptonite." *Dammit.* He closed his eyes to shake off the stupid. "What is it?"

"An extremely rare blend of isotopic alloy."

Max pursed his lips and nodded. "Ah, yes. Indeed."

"You see, my control sequence needs to absorb a massive amount of heat in order to synchronize properly. Rumac, despite his many failings, managed to develop a unique form of tungsten alloy with a colossal heat sink. He liked to use it for cooking utensils. I have not been able to replicate it." Halim dropped from the stool and hurried over to the wall of control panels. He opened a small compartment the size of a toaster oven and secured the cylinder between a pair of mounting brackets. A few swift taps closed the panel and initiated a power sequence. The metal glowed white-hot as it harnessed an enormous energy current. Halim knocked his knuckles with giddy anticipation. "Mmm, yes. Now we can have some fun."

Max scooped an armful of important-looking parts from the drive core junk pile. "Hey, do you have an incinerator I can use?"

"Yes, yes, over by the door." Halim remained fixated on the glowing cylinder.

Max sauntered over to the door, grinning at Zoey and Perra as he passed. He dropped the components into what resembled a laundry chute. An orange glow erupted from far below as the pieces met their doom. Max brushed his hands on his pants before rejoining Zoey and Perra with a smirk of satisfaction. They stood side-by-side, watching Halim from afar.

"Nicely done, Earthman," Perra said, patting him on the back.

"I must admit, pretty damn clever," Zoey said before bumping his shoulder.

Max crossed his arms and cleared his throat. "I, um, promised Halim that you two would make out for a minute when this is over."

Zoey cocked her jaw and glared at Max.

Perra snorted with laughter and covered her mouth.

Ross knocked another random object off the table. "Why won't anyone pay attention to me?!"

CHAPTER 17

Lord Essien's massive fleet assembled itself into an attack formation. Dozens of battlecruisers spread themselves around the planet, their enormous black hulls and tentacled arsenals glowing with the red hues of war. They hovered in lower orbit like the tips of monstrous arrows primed for release. The hulking barrels of plasma cannons twisted in their recesses and locked onto prime targets. The doors of missile silos slid open, allowing the eyes of nukes to peek into the black. Squadrons of Rippers swarmed around the cruisers, their spidery appendages armed and ready for the assault.

Despite the impending incursion, Hollow Hold seemed almost tranquil by comparison. Small groups of independent fighters eager to protect their sanctuary had stationed themselves around the planet. Many assumed gunner positions behind cave-protected cannons while others hid inside the interior, prepared to ambush any vessel foolish enough to enter. Numerous locals decided to flee the planet altogether, refusing to fight for an unknown cause they cared nothing about. Streaks of light carved through the green horizon as derelict ships blinked into hyperspace for parts unknown.

Orantha Nifan, on the other hand, sat inside her cozy cubby deep inside the planet's interior. Cloaked inside her silky war suit, she sipped on a fresh cocktail while awaiting the inevitable hail of Lord Essien. She glanced around her home of nine cycles, its plush interior radiating the kind of opulence that one might find in the galaxy core. Her bare feet rested upon an elaborate suede sofa. Ribbons of shimmering silk fell from her thighs and floated atop the smooth granite floor. A swanky servant offered to top off her tropical beverage, but she waved him away with a flick of her wrist. An impatient sigh escaped her lungs as she traced the rim of her glass with a ringed finger.

Varokin minions scrambled across the control bridge of Lord Essien's cruiser, shouting orders at each other as they prepared for the attack. The rumbling bellows of mounting war brought a smile to Lord Essien's face as she surveyed the bustling nerve center from above. She turned to Jai, now standing at her side in a pink tutu and matching onesie. Essien snickered at the sight, as she had every time before.

"Never gets old," she said.

Jai sighed and lowered his frowning chin.

"Silence on the bridge!" Her forceful tone ensnared the room. "I want battle prep status on my command! Nav!"

"All ships in position, Lord Essien," a random minion said.

"Resource!"

"Full capacity, m'lord."

"Arsenal!"

"Armed and ready, Your Excellency."

"Coms!"

"Links are up and awaiting instruction, m'lord."

"Excellent. Prepare for battle! Coms, establish a link to Nifan."

The com controller danced with activity, creating a cloud of static above the bridge. After a brief signal crackle, it swirled into the hologram bust of Nifan.

"Lord Essien," Nifan said with her usual indifference. "I assume you have hailed me to surrender?"

Essien snorted with sarcastic laughter and punched Jai on the shoulder. She slapped the railing a few times and wiped away imaginary tears. "Hardly, my dear. For it is I who am bestowing you that honor. One time offer. Accept it with dignity, or face annihilation."

Nifan yawned and cut the transmission.

Essien tilted her head back, unleashing the piercing eyes of indignation. "All fleet coms online!"

She stomped around the observation deck, slapping the back of Jai's head with every pass. Jai responded to each hit with a slouch of emasculation. The coms minion tapped his way across a glowing panel of fleet links, piecing together a hologram grid of cruiser captains. Essien punched Jai in the kidney on her final pass, buckling his knees. He grunted and grasped the railing, wincing in pain as she turned to address her fleet.

"Today the mighty Varokins erase the invisible hand of Orantha Nifan and destroy her poison planet! Long have we quarreled in the darkness! Long have we died at the hands of her toxic influence! It all ends, right here, right now!" She raised an open palm with crimped fingers above her head. "Ripper release! All weapons loose! On my command!"

The cruiser captains held their collective breath, awaiting the hammer drop.

Lord Essien's chest heaved with panting rage, her silvery eyes bulging from their sockets, her teeth gnashing beneath taut lips. She closed her hand into a fist and whipped her arm forward. "Attack!"

Bursts of blue light erupted from orbit as each battlecruiser unloaded its lethal arsenal. An apocalyptic rain of plasma streaks and missile trails tore through the hazy horizon. Ripper ships broke ranks and followed them down, thirsty to invade the vast cave system. Countless exhaust trails painted the dull green atmosphere with ivory brush strokes. The whites of Lord Essien's vengeful eyes reflected the hologram attack grid as the red dots of nuke missiles sped towards the caverns. Anticipating the blinding flashes and deafening rumbles of impact, she gripped the railing with both hands and leaned over the control bridge. Jai stood beside her in his pink tutu, watching the attack through a limp and deflated gaze. Lord Essien's malevolent grin grew wider, and wider, and stopped.

Nothing happened.

Red dots vanished in droves as missiles shattered into dust clouds above the surface. Plasma streaks slammed into a transparent barrier encompassing the planet, dissipating their energy into harmless dances of green light. Rippers disintegrated on impact, showering their particle remnants over the landscape. Those lucky enough to avoid a dusty fate retreated to their respective battlecruisers to regroup.

A stunned silence fell upon the control bridge as Lord Essien stared at the unscathed planet in wide-eyed disbelief. The hologram grid of cruiser captains grumbled with nervy confusion. Varokin minions shot bewildered glances at each other, then to Lord Essien, then to the planet, then back to each other. All eyes turned to the planet surface as faint orange glows arose from the cavern depths. Moments later, thousands upon thousands of white exhaust trails lifted from the caves as legions of missiles screamed towards their targets.

Essien's jaw dropped. "Fuck."

* * *

Halim bounced and clapped his hands as the barrage of missiles tore Lord Essien's armada to shreds. The group stood around a large hologram projection of the planet, cast from the ceiling into the open air above the floor. It bathed the group in a yellow sheen as they studied the countless icons swirling around the surface. Red triangles represented battlecruisers while orange circles identified Rippers. White dots had denoted the plasma and missile strikes before the planetary defense system rendered them futile. Blue dots revealed the counter-assault, rising from the hologram sphere like a flower shedding pollen. Red and orange icons disappeared in waves as the swarm of blue dots hunted them down, much to the delight of a giddy Halim. He threw his arms up and cheered as the final red triangle blipped out of existence.

"A total success!" Halim said.

Perra placed a hand over her mouth and glanced at Zoey, who stood motionless with her arms crossed. Max studied the holographic annihilation with the tilted head of a puzzled dog. Ross radiated his usual indifference, batting at whatever icon floated into his vicinity. Bursting with pride and glee, Halim pranced over to the control panel wall. A few swift taps summoned Nifan, using multiple panels to create a larger image.

"Greetings, Master Halim. I trust the news is good?"

"Utter destruction, Madam Nifan. Every ship destroyed, every blast contained, every missile reduced to dust. And, might I add, all without a single blemish to the planet. I am happy to confirm that my planetary defense system worked perfectly, as expected."

Nifan grinned. "Very impressive. You are a true gem, Master Halim."

"I also extend my deepest gratitude for allowing me the opportunity to test it properly."

"You are most welcome, and I will see to it personally that you are handsomely rewarded for your effort. And please pass along my regards to our esteemed guests."

"I will, Madam Nifan. A good day to you."

"And to you as well." Nifan offered a slight bow before the transmission ended.

Halim sighed with contentment. "Madam Nifan would like to thank you—" he said, turning to face the group, but found the open barrel of Zoey's plasma gun.

She pulled the trigger.

The ear-splitting blast incinerated his head and carved a large black crater into the wall behind him. Rumbles of impact echoed around the chamber and jostled the floor beneath their feet. Shards of charred electronics scattered themselves across the room. Machine parts rattled upon the tables and fell to the floor. Lighting panels flickered as static charges snaked across a mangled mess of exposed wiring. Smoke enveloped the immediate area and dissipated into the flowing air vents. Halim's headless body and cauterized neck fell forward and slapped the tile at Zoey's feet. She took a gratified breath, lowered her weapon, and turned her attention to the group. Perra and Max stood frozen with contrasting expressions of horror. Ross trembled where he stood as a poofed ball of orange fur.

Zoey shrugged. "What? You do know that was *Halim*, right?"

Max placed a hand over his heart and lowered to a knee.

Perra regained her composure and swiped some debris from her shoulder. "Yeah, but that was a bit cavalier, don't you think?"

"That was badass," Ross said, still poofed and shaking.

"I think the cat's in shock," Zoey said.

"Can you blame him?" Max said, completing his slow descent to the floor. "You went all Trinity on us. You could have at least warned us with a 'dodge this' or something."

"Who?" Perra said.

"I'll explain later," Max said. "Right now I need to get my heart back down to a billion beats a minute."

"Bad ... ass ..." Ross fell to his knees and thumped face-first onto the floor.

"Kitty down," Max said, assuming zero responsibility.

"You're all a bunch of babies," Zoey said.

She nabbed a pair of pliers from Halim's pocket and stepped over to the control panel wall. With the thrust of an elbow, she shattered the glass compartment containing the cylinder. She reached inside with the pliers, plucked it from the brackets, and walked it over to the incinerator. A flick of the wrist cast the cylinder into oblivion, resulting in a brief orange glow. Zoey smirked at the sight, signaling an official end to their perilous quest. Strolling up from behind, Perra dropped her chin on Zoey's shoulder and hugged her waist. Zoey leaned her head against Perra's and stroked her cheek, evoking a pair of contented smiles as they stared down into the chute.

"Love you," Perra said in a soft voice.

"Love you too."

"Can we go now?"

"Absolutely."

Perra kissed Zoey's cheek and released her grip. They turned to their companions, still recovering on the floor in various positions of distress.

"I'll get the cat," Perra said and lumbered forward.

* * *

The tiny freighter lifted over the rim of a giant cave entrance, bringing Hollow Hold's sun-drenched landscape into full view. A wave of natural light squinted eyes and warmed skins. Chunks of the ravaged assault fleet burned up in the atmosphere, creating a twinkling rain. Numerous ships engaged their thrusters and floated into the cavern depths, returning home after receiving word of the battle victory. Zoey reached across the control panel and took Perra's hand, who returned a loving smile.

"If this whole experience has taught me anything," Zoey said while scanning the jagged landscape, "it's that I never want to see this rancid shitbox ever again."

"Agreed," Perra said.

"Ditto," Max said.

"I dunno, the core was nice," Ross said.

Max punched his thigh, prompting a brief slap fight with grunts and hisses.

"Children!" Zoey said.

Max and Ross settled down and glared at each other.

"On that note, let's get the hell out of here," Perra said.

"With pleasure."

Zoey slid an open palm up the console, igniting the main engines. The ship rumbled into the sky, punched through the atmosphere, and sailed into the blackness of space.

"Coordinates set?" Zoey said.

"Locked and loaded," Perra said.

"Where are we going?" Max said.

"Anywhere but here." Zoey slapped the jump drive icon, enveloping the ship in a sliver of purple light.

* * *

A small, silvery capsule floated nearby, hanging above the Hollow Hold horizon like a crippled satellite. Its egg-shaped hull reflected the flash of the freighter's departure. Inside the one-man escape pod, Lord Essien faced Jai Ferenhal, who still wore his pink tutu and matching onesie. Essien squirmed inside the cramped compartment, trying to gain some wiggle room. She groaned with frustration and headbutted Jai in the chest. He dropped his meaty chin and scowled at her, lobbing hateful insults without saying a word. Essien heaved and writhed before pausing to examine a peculiar odor. Her face crumpled with disgust as she glared up at Jai.

"You're such an asshole."

CHAPTER 18

Max awoke to the rattling purr of a furry mound atop his chest. Contented breaths flowed through his nostrils as sleepy eyes scanned the dim bedchamber. He lifted a hand off the covers and stroked Ross's back, prompting a grumpy moan and some invasive stretching. Max shifted his head from side to side to avoid the invading paws, but ended up with a mouthful of fur anyway. Ross retracted his wayward limbs and rewrapped them into a fuzzy pile. Max grimaced and spat out a few hairs.

"Good to have you back, buddy," Max said.

"From what?" Ross said, half asleep.

"Nevermind." Max yawned and smacked his lips. His stomach grumbled, signaling a long-neglected need. "I guess it's been a while. You hungry?"

"I don't need to eat, jackass."

"But you *do* eat."

"That doesn't mean I get hungry."

"So how do you know when you need to eat?"

"I *just* told you that I *don't* need to eat."

"Oh. But ... hmm."

Ross tilted his head and glared at Max. "Are you having another episode? Do I need to seek shelter?"

"No, I'm fine. Just a little groggy, I guess." Max reached into the crisp, cool air and cupped his hands behind his head. The stillness of the room allowed his mind to wander. He replayed the events of the previous days, retracing the fantastical journey from Earth to Europa, from Andromeda to Hollow Hold. A wide smile puckered his cheeks. "That was an interesting adventure."

"Mmhmm."

Max dropped his chin and frowned at Ross. "That's your entire summation?"

"What do you want me to say? That it was a life-changing experience full of magic, wonder, and blah blah blah?"

"Was it not?"

Ross cocked his ears. "Where is this going?"

Max rolled his eyes. "Nowhere, apparently. Forget about it, Garfield."

"That's racist."

Max chuckled, then scooped the feline with both hands and set him aside. Ross lifted into an arched stretch, greeting the day as every cat does. Max whipped the covers away and swung his legs out from the bed. His bare feet pressed into the cold metal floor, prompting an involuntary shiver.

"Denchi."

Strips of LEDs responded to the command, illuminating the gray interior. Max dropped his face into both hands and rubbed his tired eyes. A grunting stretch left him limp and ready for whatever the day threw at him. He turned his attention to the rear wall.

"What's that transparency command?"

"Um ... fikarek," Ross said.

The wall replaced itself with a bright cityscape, pouring the combined light of three small suns into the cabin. Max cringed and lifted a hand to block the light while his eyes adjusted.

"Oh, uh, what's the word ..." Ross said. "Nuicha."

The wall dimmed a bit as if the room had donned a pair of sunglasses. Max lowered his arm, allowing his bewildered eyes to digest the alien landscape. The tiny freighter had settled upon a row of landing platforms, all stony gray with yellow safety rails. Immaculate ships with burnished hulls rested on the pads, featuring sleek designs and elaborate detailing, the spacefaring equivalent of luxury yachts. Each platform connected to an enormous gangway that led into the city. Countless humanoids plodded down the promenade in every direction. Some dressed in trendy attire while others made use of natural attire. The white hulls of shuttles raced overhead, transporting their occupants to parts unknown. Glittering towers punched through the cloudbank. Their silvery sidings reflected the cool blues of the atmosphere, rendering them ethereal. Three looming suns bathed the city in a radiant light that reminded Max of home.

"Where are we?" Max said.

"Don't know exactly," Ross said. "Somewhere inside Andromeda."

"Wow." He huffed and shook his head. "And to think we were sitting on Earth a few days ago."

"Do you miss it?"

"I, um ... I don't really know."

Ross smirked.

Max sighed and bowed his head. "I had a dream last night. Nothing interesting, just some mundane crap back on Earth, but it made me realize something. Over the last several days, we have seen and done some crazy shit. If I had known what we were getting ourselves into, I would have never left the basement." He lifted a solemn gaze and stared at his muddied reflection on the wall. "And that's the big damn shame of it all. I would have stayed. I wanted out, more than anything in the world, but I would have stayed."

"And yet, here we are."

Max grinned and nodded. "And here we are. Funny thing is, despite all the stress and chaos, I've never felt so at peace. I think I'm happy, truly happy, for the first time in my life." He turned to Ross. "You've been my only real friend over the last decade. To be honest, I can't think of a single person I actually miss. I've known Zoey and Perra for less than a week, and I care more about them than I do my own joyless family. That's when it hit me. I never really had a family until now."

Ross snapped out of a boredom trance. "I'm sorry, what? I was thinking about bacon."

Max chuckled. "Nothing, forget about it."

He lifted from the bed, spruced himself up, and slipped into a clean set of clothes. Refreshed, and with an empty stomach in desperate need of attention, Max opened the cabin door and entered the cargo bay. He scanned the room and marveled at the cleanliness; every surface scrubbed and polished, every net and container restored to its proper position.

"Hey there, sleepyhead," Perra said as she hung a tool inside a locker. Also refreshed, she wore a clean set of punky attire, complete with purple corset, bronze leather straps, and gunmetal buckles atop a cropped leather skirt. Her worn boots clanked on the clean floor as she walked over to greet him.

"Hey, yourself," Max said as they embraced.

"How are you feeling?"

"Okay, I guess. Can't believe I slept through entry."

"I can, considering what we went through. You passed out hard, my friend."

"I guess I needed it." Max rubbed his neck. "So where are we?"

"Marcoza, a neutral planet deep in the heart of Andromeda. It's also the headquarters for the Council of Loken peacekeepers. Zoey is over there right now filing a report on our escapade. Should be back any tick. Oh, and if you're hungry, we picked up a load of fresh rations. They're in the back whenever you're ready."

"Oh thank goodness, you read my mind."

"I've already eaten, so dig right in."

"Morning," Ross said as he trotted into the bay.

Perra kneeled down and scratched his head. "And a good morning to you too."

Ross purred for a moment, then launched into a spontaneous grooming session.

Max strolled to the rear of the cargo bay where a bundle of cloth bags and cardboard boxes housed an impressive amount of eating options. His mouth began to salivate as his eyes surveyed the bounty; colorful fruits and vegetables, an array of cured meats, cans of mystery items, and bottles of cloudy liquids. He nabbed a squishy purple fruit resting on top, its skin covered in small bumps and a dense brown fuzz. Having no idea what constituted proper consumption, he shrugged and bit into the flesh. His eyelids collapsed under the weight of ecstasy as sweet yellow nectar dripped into his hand. "Holy mother of mayhem, that's incredible." He devoured the decadent fruit, licked his hand clean, and continued his sampling fiesta. Strips of this, handfuls of that, just a ravenous glutton indulging in a well-earned bout of hedonism.

Stuffed and satisfied beyond words, Max shuffled through the cargo bay while licking his fingertips. The airlock door slid open as he neared the cockpit, revealing a gorgeous Zoey in a striking black suit. Her choppy black hair flowed to one side under a sheen of product. The gray pinstripes of her jacket and slacks fell to an elegant pair of strappy shoes. The image caught Max by surprise, his eyes drinking her body from head to toe with a finger still inside his mouth.

"That's not creepy at all," Zoey said as she stepped inside.

"Oh, sorry," Max said, averting his eyes. "You just look, well, stunning."

"Thanks."

"Not that you didn't before, or anything. You know."

"Thanks."

"Because you did. Not that I looked. Don't want you to think that I, well, yeah."

Zoey narrowed her eyes.

Max scratched his head and glanced away. "Is this the tweak?"

"The what?"

"The, um ... thing." (It wasn't. A local flower had become hilariously carnivorous.)

"Okay, you can stop now."

"Fair enough." Max leaned down to pet the cat.

Ross jerked away. "Piss off, muppet. I'm not a life raft for your social ineptitude."

"Fine." Max stood with his arms raised. "I'll just get myself another weirdly delicious hair-fruit."

Zoey snickered as Max clanked away.

Perra emerged from the cockpit. "So how'd it go?"

"Pretty well, actually. They were sympathetic to the plight, commended us for our bravery and such. Apart from that, just a bunch of bureaucratic questioning. Major players, timeline, ship codes, favorite color, all that crap. The big takeaway is that we have no liability. We are free to go about our business."

"Excellent. And for the record, you do look stunning in that suit." Perra winked.

Zoey smirked in reply. "Speaking of business, the PCDS gave us another package to deliver." She lifted a square box about the same size as before.

Perra recoiled a bit.

"Don't worry," Zoey said. "I already asked. It's a bunch of rare stones for a specialized jeweler out in Ursa Major."

"That we can do," Perra said, then leaned in for a kiss.

Max returned while munching on a piece of fuzzy fruit. Zoey and Perra smiled at each other and turned to the human.

"Earth is on the way to Ursa Major," Zoey said. "We can drop you off. Or, you can stay here on Marcoza and catch a jump shuttle. Your choice."

Max paused for thought, but kept chewing.

"Or ..." Perra said, taking Zoey's hand, "you can stick around and be my grease monkey protégé. To be honest, we could use the extra hand."

Max ruffled his brow and strolled to the open airlock. He leaned on the frame, took another bite, and studied the colorful creatures tromping along the gangway. A fog of foreign aromas teased his nostrils, drawing a cheeky grin. His gaze climbed the shimmering towers and wandered through the cloudbank. Max chuckled to himself as a transport shuttle sailed overhead.

"Ross, what do you th—"

"Don't care," Ross said while licking his extended leg.

"Then it's settled." Max slapped the wall panel and the airlock door slid shut. "We got a package to deliver."

About the Author

Zachry Wheeler is an award-winning science fiction novelist, screenwriter, and coffee slayer. He enjoys English football, stand-up comedy, and is known to lurk around museums and brewpubs.

Learn more at ZachryWheeler.com.

Works by the Author

Immortal Wake Series

Transient
Thursday Midnight
The Mortal Vestige

Max and the Multiverse Series

Max and the Multiverse
Max and the Snoodlecock
Max and the Banjo Ferret

Max and the Multiverse Shorts

The Item of Monumental Importance
Nibblenom Deathtrap
Sparkle Pirate

Before You Go

If you enjoyed this book, please consider posting a short review on Amazon. Ratings and reviews are the currency by which authors gain visibility. They are the single greatest way to show your support and keep us writing the stories that you love.

Thank you for reading!

Made in the USA
Middletown, DE
04 August 2020